NULL
— and —
VOID

Book 1 of the Last Kitsune

J.S. Scheffel

PAGE PUBLISHING
Conneaut Lake, PA

First originally published by Page Publishing 2023

ISBN 979-8-88960-040-4 (pbk)
ISBN 979-8-88960-049-7 (digital)

Printed in the United States of America

CHAPTER 1

It had been a particularly long and grueling shift, but I was in the final stretch and just feet from being able to face plant onto my bed. Fatigue seemed to weigh my limbs as I rested my forehead on the steering wheel. Raising my head, I admired the sunrise as it cast a shadow across the newly painted bungalow. My parents left it to me after retiring to the old country, aka Tampa. I contrasted the light beige siding color with a splash of eggplant on the trim. The pop of color never failed to make me smile. However, my smile turned into a grimace when my eyes lit on a small hunched woman as she pulled a large planter through the bungalow door. Sighing deeply, I slowly left the cramped confines of my old Suzuki X90 and quietly approached her.

"Uka, we've talked about this. It is still too cold outside for this plant. It's just going to die if you keep dragging it out of the house," I said, amazed that this older woman had the strength to handle the ceramic pot. She'd gifted it to me the week before, and I'd been struggling with her ever since.

"Plant belongs outside door to protect house. Inside, will cause trouble." Shrewd brown eyes looked up at me as my petite neighbor struggled with the pot holding the Saint George sword plant. She often treated me as a rather dimwitted granddaughter.

Sighing, I helped her move it into place and shook my head. "Fine. But I don't want to hear about it if it dies."

Taking my hand in hers, she patted it gently. "It will not die. It is one of Uka's plants. Very strong."

I smiled and wrapped the small Japanese woman in a hug. She barely reached my collarbone. But what she lacked in height, she more than made up for in what my father would have called grit. Looking down into her friendly wrinkled face, I kissed her head and let her go. Waving over her shoulder, she walked along the well-worn path between our houses. Her yard already contained a riot of growth, even though it was still early in April. I could see daffodils, snowdrops, and hyacinths adding color to the edges of her walkway. I looked forward to the coming weeks when I would become the beneficiary of her vegetable garden.

Biting back a yawn, I entered the house through the open door and found my roommate staring from the shadows of the front bedroom.

"Why did you let Uka carry that thing outside?"

Nico shrugged. "It's not like I could run out and stop her, Tai. She opened all the blinds and let the sun in."

That was the problem with having a vampire for a roommate. Although he could be awake during the day, any exposure to sunlight would severely burn him. Our elderly neighbor seemed to take advantage of that, though she only knew that Nico had an "allergy" to the sun. Vampires and other Supernaturals were still in the closet. I was considered a Null—someone born of Supernatural parents but who have no powers of their own. Nulls could easily pass for humans and often lived among them. But even Nulls benefited from the magical genes. I was stronger and faster than my human contemporaries, and my eyesight was keener. It all worked to my advantage as a paramedic. It was nothing for me to wrestle a two-hundred-pound man onto a backboard, and I could see minor changes in a patient's breathing or color long before any instrument registered a problem. I did have to play it down and be cautious since I worked with an all-human crew. But I'd had no interest in working in the Supernatural world and wanted as little to do with it as possible except for Nico. We'd been friends since school, and I couldn't imagine life without his neurotic presence.

"What are you still doing up?" I asked him as I moved through the small house, closing the blinds.

He followed as close behind as he could and avoided any stray shafts of light. I wandered into the kitchen and turned to find 150 pounds of vampire breathing down my neck.

"What is your issue?" I asked. I grabbed the pot off the coffee maker, stopping long enough to drop my work jacket on the nearest chair. Turning to the sink to fill it, I tried to ignore my roommate, who was still mere inches away.

"I have no idea what you're talking about," he said, his voice squeaking a bit.

Now here is a fact. I know books and television would have you believe that vampires are these alpha predators, all sleek and deadly, and some of them are. Then there's Nico. Anyone meeting him for the first time would take him for a computer nerd. They would be right. He is tall and thin, has slightly hunched shoulders, and makes a lot of money programming computers. But his true joy comes from being an impersonator slash drag queen. See where I'm going here? It's hard to take a vampire seriously when you've seen them made up like Judy Garland and singing "Somewhere Over the Rainbow." He is the mildest-tempered (wimpy) nerd in town when he is not in one of his drag personas. Or at least in this neighborhood. But he is good-looking in that androgynous way that many of his kind are.

Leaning on the counter, I set the coffeepot down safely, though not so far away I couldn't grab it and throw it at my friend if the need arose. I knew that tone of voice. That was his "I need something from you, and you're not going to like it" tone. The last time he used that, I had to dress up as Ethel Merman and lip-synch my way through "I Got Rhythm." Long story, don't ask.

"Spit it out. What do you want now?"

Keeping his eyes on the countertop as if the random pattern of color was the most fascinating thing he had ever seen. He cleared his throat and tried to sound casual. "It's really nothing. I have a small party and wanted you to go with me."

Since men and women flock around him at the club where he performs most nights, he could easily convince any of them to go with him. There could only be one reason he wanted me to go; it involved people (and I use the term lightly) to whom he couldn't introduce a human.

Peeling one eye open, I saw that there had been no movement and that sad little vampire was still in my kitchen, giving me a hopeful look. I closed my eyes and prayed that if I stood like that long enough, he would lose interest and wander away. A girl can have dreams, can't she?

His eyes pleaded with me. "I swear, it's just a tiny, itsy-bitsy cocktail party. Hardly anyone will be there. Just a few hotshots have flown in for the gathering. You know, it will be mostly small talk. Hardly any politics at all. We'll be in and out in a flash. You don't have to talk to anyone except me and maybe my mother." The last few words were mumbled, and I had to ask him to repeat them several times to make sure I heard right.

"Your mother?" I repeated. "The same woman who represents the House of Rodrick on the High Council? *That* mother?"

"Please, please, please. Mummy has been on me for ages about my life. Who are my friends? What am I doing with my life?"

"Really? You did not just refer to your vampire mother as Mummy!" I bit my lip. But hard as I tried, I couldn't stop the snort of laughter that escaped.

Deciding that this conversation was not worth breaking my coffeepot over his head, I poured the water into the coffee maker. Grabbing the decaf from the shelf over the counter, I scoop just enough into the filter to make one final robust cup before bed.

"So she will find your Null friend an acceptable date for her precious son?"

"Well, it's not like I have a lot of choices now." Nico's voice fell to a whisper.

Guilt had me turning to him and giving him a one-armed hug. I'd forgotten that his relationship with Peter, the very human owner of the club where he performed, was still new and shiny and very much on the down-low. Peter was also unaware of my roommate's, let's say, peculiar diet. I hope Councilwoman Roderick was not expecting a load of grandkids anytime soon.

Too exhausted to argue, I said, "I'll think about it. Just let me get some sleep first, okay?"

Brightening noticeably, he hugged me back and kissed my cheek. The smile he gave me only made me feel worse. "You're the best. Now get some sleep. I'd hate to see bags under those beautiful eyes."

Watching as he turned and almost skipped into his room, I had this horrible feeling that I was missing something.

Five hours later, it occurred to me what I had missed. I should have asked Nico when this party was happening. Note to self: start locking the bedroom door.

"Explain to me again why you had to wake me up at four o'clock," I asked as I sat on the edge of my bed, blinking.

"Maybe if you had gone straight to bed this morning instead of reading until all hours, you would have gotten enough sleep. Now we only have four hours to find you something to wear, do your nails, style your hair, and do something with those things you call eyebrows," Nico said as he dove headfirst into my closet.

I leaned to the side as he flung clothes at me. Magoo, my twenty-pound myopic tabby, hissed and jumped off the bed, relinquishing his spot to the pile of clothes and hangers forming next to me. Grabbing my phone from next to the bed, I gave in to temptation and snapped a picture of Nico, butt in the air, as he started in on my shoes.

"Just as I thought. Nothing, absolutely nothing. Do you even own any dresses or heels? Never mind, stay here."

I flopped back on the bed and stared at the ceiling, taking stock of my life. It had been two years since my adoptive parents had retired to Florida and left me with the house. It was paid off, and all I needed to worry about were the taxes and upkeep. But after a few weeks of living alone, I decided that I needed more than my eleven-year-old cat to talk to and invited my best friend to move in. Having been friends since our early teens, this would be a great solution. I forgot what a diva he could be. Being one of his only friends privy to his lifestyle, he was free to be the pushy fashionista he was born to be. All Supes were in the metaphorical closet, but he took that to a new

5

extreme. I'm not sure he would ever see the light of day. (See what I did there? Vampire? Light of day?)

Nico charged back into the room, his arms stacked high with dresses and shoeboxes. He picked up the previous conversation as if he had never left the room." And we've got to get you something to eat before we go. I do not need a hangry Tai attacking the buffet. It will be like your fifteenth birthday party all over again."

"Hey!" That had led to an all-out, uncontrolled food fight. I swear, I found my mom's liver sausage spread in random places for days afterward. "If you hadn't tried to take that cupcake away from me, I wouldn't have smashed your face into the spinach dip."

"Whatever, here try this and this and…no, forget this one. Maybe if we…? No, then we'd have to…" I tuned out his muttering while clothes and shoes were sorted. Holding my arms out to my sides, he held items up and scrutinized the intended result. Pieces were discarded left and right until all that was left was an eighties-style tube dress in a black material that sparkled in the light. However, I drew the line at the 4" black CFM heels he selected and chose a wedge instead.

After a century of being groomed and styled, Nico declared me fit to be seen in public and wandered off to take care of himself. All that was left was finding the right jewelry to complete my transformation. I rummaged through some of the things my mother had left behind, found a delicate diamond solitaire necklace, and added some simple hoops for my ears. I slipped on the gold bracelet I wore on special occasions. It featured a charm made of jade in the shape of a heart and had the word *Taisetsuna* engraved on the surface. The term was Japanese for "treasured one," which is the name the supernatural version of DCFS decided to give me when I was found.

I saw the picture of my adoptive parents, Hank and Rachel Jotuns. Not a day passed that I was not thankful for their love and desire to adopt a Null of unknown origin. My father was a Milwaukee cop at the time. Being the first on the scene of a car fire, he discovered me on the side of the road, unharmed, except for a deep gash across the palm of my left hand. He immediately sensed the "other" on me. They assumed I had been in the car, but the only other occupant was burnt beyond recognition, little more than a pile of ash. Nothing remained that could help identify me except for a charm that I now wore around my wrist. I don't remember any of it since I was less than two years old. But my mother told me how she fell in love with me that night. My father convinced the authorities to let him and Rachel care for me until other arrangements could be made. Those other arrangements ended up consisting of my being placed with the Alpha of the local shifter community for the next three years.

At five years old, most Supernaturals, especially shifters, will begin exhibiting some of their parents' qualities. Some children can start shifting at that time, and even Nulls will at least begin showing some traits humans would consider extraordinary. But I never developed any of those. Doctors, witches, and shamans were all brought in to examine me. There was nothing wrong with me, physically. They could all sense the "otherness" that marked me different from humans. But when a classmate in my kindergarten class accidentally broke my arm playing, it was decided that I was best off in a different environment. So Hank and Rachel swooped in and raised me as their own. Both of my parents were of Germanic forest troll ancestry, not the "hiding under a bridge and eating innocent billy goats" kind, and the line had been diluted enough that they could pass as human. Feeling it essential to embrace my Supernatural heritage, they eventually enrolled me in the Maxwell Academy, where Supes from all over the world sent their children. That was where I met my BFF and had my heart broken for the first time.

Facing the full-length mirror that hung from the back of my bedroom door, I looked at the image of the woman I had become. Average height but with legs that seemed longer than they should be in this dress. Curves in the correct places and no bulges showing, thanks to all the exercise I got at work. All in all, Nico had done an excellent job. My brown eyes had a slight cast that hinted at my Asian heritage. But the rest of me screamed European. Even my hair, worn short for easy styling, was a dark red that was not quite auburn and had dark brown (almost black) lowlights running through it. He had managed to underscore my best qualities without overdoing them. Subtle shading highlighted cheekbones that my oval face customarily obscured. No eyeshadow graced my face, but he had produced a cat's-eye look that I could never accomplish on my own. My hair was fluffed, curled, and sprayed to within an inch of its life, but it still looked soft.

Quietly making my way to the kitchen, I discreetly made a small sandwich and poured myself a glass of milk. Nico was correct; I could be a real bitch when hungry. But I didn't want him to see me eating. It would set bad precedence if he found out he was right about something. Also, this was the first time in years that other Supes would surround me, and I was jumpy. I still had a few Null friends, but for the most part, I avoided contact with most Supernaturals and shifters, particularly since that incident at the junior/senior prom. After ten years, I still was not ready to run into anyone I used to know. Maybe a valium would do more for me than milk.

The sound of someone clearing their throat startled me enough that I choked on a mouthful of food.

Turning my most innocent look on him, I told Nico, "It's not how it looks. I was feeling faint from all the hairspray fumes and decided it would help to have something in my stomach."

My mouth fell open in astonishment. If I thought my transformation was astounding, it had nothing on Nico's. Dark hair slicked back, he was rocking an old-school tuxedo. It was black with a long jacket over a satin vest. His fingers tugged nervously at the starched collar.

"Whoa, dude. Who died and made you Dracula?"

"Whatever," he replied, holding my good wool coat out for me. While it was technically spring, the evenings in Wisconsin were still quite cool.

"And do *not* put up that hood. Goodness only knows what your hair would look like, and I won't present myself with some street urchin," he proclaimed as we made our way to the garage. He always turned into a nineteenth-century autocrat when he was nervous.

I stuck my tongue out at his retreating back and wobbled carefully behind him. Wedges might have been a better choice, but I was not used to wearing heels. My usual footwear consisted of my work boots and flats or flip-flops, and I still managed to trip over thin air in those.

We took his car so our clothing would not be dirtied by my vintage (old) Suzuki. I settled back in my seat and enjoyed the scenery I was usually too tired to notice. Century-old bungalows rubbed shoulders with grand Victorians and brick duplexes as we headed through the neighborhood and toward our destination. Cresting the top of the Hoan Harbor bridge, I admired the lights of Milwaukee as they shimmered on the smooth lake surface. Too soon, we exited the highway, heading into the heart of downtown. I rarely made it into town. I always felt claustrophobic among the towering buildings and crowds of people. But this night, the streets seemed almost deserted. Harp-styled streetlights shed more atmospheric than helpful light on the avenues and buildings. Nico's car glided almost soundlessly and stopped in from of a brick-fronted building. A parking valet stepped forward to take his car keys. Nico took my elbow and escorted me to the smoked glass doors with the word *Verge* written in fancy script in the bottom right corner. The steady pulse from a bass guitar was the only sound that disturbed the early spring evening as we took our first steps through the doors.

CHAPTER 2

Stepping into a small foyer, we were greeted by some of the largest Supes to pass for humans, mountain trolls. These backwoods cousins of mine were big and scary but relatively slow in the mental department. Nearly seven feet tall, neither wore any shoes with their jeans and monogrammed shirts. If I had one thing in common with my adopted kin, I preferred to be barefoot. That could be problematic this time of year since I did not have the traditional hairy feet.

Nico silently handed over an embossed card to the closest of the duo. After squinting at it and sniffing it, he tossed it over his shoulder and opened another set of doors to let us into the inner sanctum (I presumed).

Walking a couple of steps behind my roommate, I overheard the troll that had handled the card murmur something in his companion's ear. I was very familiar with trollish slang, and he had called me something akin to a "blood whore" for being with a vampire. I quickly turned, standing on my tiptoes, and pointed my finger at his face. "Dunker Bronzebeard, you shut your mouth before I call your mother and tell her that her son cannot behave in public."

Leaning down to get a closer look at my face (did I forget to mention that mountain trolls have bad eyesight), he paled noticeably. "I'm sorry, Cousin Tai. I didn't recognize you."

"Well, on behalf of all women, I refuse your apology. You know better than that. Aunt Hodag would tan your hide if she were here."

"Please, Cousin Tai, don't tell Ma," my other cousin pleaded.

"Don't think I didn't hear you snicker, Sunreaver. You would be in just as much trouble." I stood back and relaxed my pose. Not because I was done but because I was getting the mother of all cramps in my calves.

"I might be persuaded to forget this little misunderstanding if you came to take down that dead tree in my backyard." You never just forgave a troll. Penance must be demanded after an insult. Otherwise, they would see you as weak, and if there is one thing you don't want, it is for a mountain troll to think you're weak. Cousins or not.

"Yes, Cousin Tai," they chorused while avoiding my gaze. Big and scary as they were, there was nothing worse you could threaten them than telling their mother on them.

I limped over to where Nico waited for me. At the sight of his raised eyebrow, I just shrugged and shooed with both hands. The sooner we got in, the sooner I could get home. My grateful eyes fell on a well-stocked bar at the far end of the dimly lit room we had just entered. Leaving Nico behind, I made a straight path to it. All the pain in my legs was forgotten.

Deafening music pulsed through my body as I waited for the tall thin shifter behind the bar to take my drink order. Turning to survey the room, I realized how lucky I had been to make it to the polished oak bar without being trampled. I don't remember the last time I had been amid so many different Supernaturals. There must have been over a dozen shifters on the dance floor alone. Vamps stayed in the shadows, sipping drinks that looked suspiciously like blood as they mingled with other night creatures, one of which looked an awful lot like a ghoul. Glancing up, I saw fairies in their natural forms hovering overhead around specially built tables suspended from the ceiling.

In the time I spent taking in our surroundings, Nico had made it to the bar and leaned over to yell in my ear, "What do you want to drink?"

"Get me a whiskey sour please. With a bib." The bib was not in case I spilled the drink on myself, though that is always possible. It was a way of letting the bartender know only to make it human strength. If I allowed myself to begin tipping back drinks made for Supes, I would be on the floor by midnight.

Placing our drinks in front of us, the bartender leaned over to hear what Nico was saying. His change was accompanied by a gesture toward the back of the room. Turning to look, I could make out elevator doors.

Grabbing our drinks, we pushed our way through the crowd of people that had suddenly appeared behind us. Amazingly, the doors opened once we got within five feet, and we hurried into the waiting lift. Leaning against the back wall, I rubbed my forehead as a music-induced headache began to recede. The doors had nearly shut when a highly polished black loafer forced its way between them, and they stopped. What followed next was stuff out of my nightmares and the first strike of the evening.

"Well, if it isn't Null and Void and her little vampire pet," said a voice all too high pitched to be coming from the hulking wolf shifter in front of us.

Pain pierced my heart at the sound of that high school nickname. But unlike the first (and last) time Stefan had uttered it, I did not break his nose. I had grown up a bit (or not, the night was young).

Before I could come up with a witty and scathing reply, strike 2 followed behind him. At just six and a half feet tall, Ash Montgomery was everything my heart ever desired—until he rejected me and threw me to the wolves. Dressed in tight black jeans and a black silk shirt, his otherness seemed to radiate from him, from his amber-colored eyes to his collar-length golden hair. He didn't walk so much as stalk into the confined space of the elevator, scanning each corner until his eyes landed on me. I noticed fine lines at the corner of his eyes as he smiled.

"Taisetsuna, it has been too long. Are you in town for the conference?" His deep smoky voice sent shivers down my spine, just like they had ten years prior and every year before that.

I tried my best to sound cool and detached. "I'm in town because I live here."

"I thought you had gone off somewhere for college?" he replied.

"That was years ago, and I've been back home for a long time." Once upon a time, we had been close, and it hurt me a little that he hadn't cared enough to track where I was or how I was doing. I knew everything he had been up to, thanks to gossip central (aka Nico). I knew he had turned down the Beta position in our local pack and started his own security company, a company that had just gone public and whose shares were skyrocketing.

"I'm surprised I haven't seen you around town."

"That's because she works too much and has no life," Nico chimed in.

Resisting the urge to smack my BFF on top of his head, I smiled tightly. "I'm a paramedic. The long hours don't leave me much time to get out."

That was a complete lie. I worked twenty-four hours on duty and forty-eight off, which left me plenty of time. But I often found myself happily working around the house or helping Uka with her garden.

Thankfully we had reached our floor before I had to field any other awkward questions. Ash held the doors open for us, and I let Nico go ahead of me. Following behind, I felt a hand on the small of my back as another discreetly slid up my thigh. Startled, I stepped back on Stefan's foot and swung around, letting my closed fist strike him in the balls. Total accident, I swear. That's my story, and I'm sticking to it.

"Oh my gosh, I am so sorry." Feigning shock, I gasped and covered my mouth. "You startled me. I hope I didn't hurt you."

Stefan's eyes glowed gold as he bared his teeth and fought back his wolf. "I'm fine. Just a misunderstanding."

Ash narrowed his eyes as he looked at us both. "I'm sure it was. Stefan, give the guards their details and cover the back exit."

So he must be in charge of security tonight. That only made sense since I had heard (again, through Nico) that his company, Bagha, worked in both the human and Supe communities. The name was fitting, as it was Hindi for "tiger," Ash's shifter form. It was also a nod to his Hindu ancestry on his mother's side.

Stefan shot me a look so full of loathing I was sure I had made an actual enemy that evening.

Once out of sight, Ash turned to me. "Would you care to tell me what that was all about?"

"Nothing that concerns you, Ash. I'm sure you have more important things to deal with," I snapped.

I had known Ash from the time I was in the care of the pack after the car wreck. He had always watched over me, and he was the one that had carried me to the pack house when a careless shifter child had broken my arm while we played. I worshipped him after that. If only he had shown this same concern ten years ago at our school prom, I might not be standing there trying to hold back the hurt, humiliation, and betrayal I still felt, hurt that sixteen-year-old Tai had confessed her feelings for a then eighteen-year-old Ash and had them rejected, tossed aside, as if I couldn't possibly know my mind at that age. I was humiliated that he had done it in front of all his friends and betrayed that he had practically pushed me at Stefan and ordered him to take me home after tossing his car keys to him.

Maybe I should be thanking him, however. Because of that ride home and Stefan's wandering hands, I could finally tap into some of the Supe energy that everyone else I knew had. It had come rushing out of me after I had pried myself out of Stefan's grasp and jumped from the car. Standing and shaking in my driveway, I had been groped and verbally abused by that adolescent boy. Stefan told me that Ash had obviously "given" me to him and how I should be grateful that anyone would want to be with a worthless orphan, a "Null and Void" like me. All I remember after that was throwing myself at him, kicking and screaming. I had felt as if my whole body was on fire, and before I knew it, I had broken his nose and doubled him over with a vicious kick to the balls (I'm sensing a pattern here).

Hearing the commotion, my parents came running out of the house. My mother comforted me while my father had Stefan in the air by his throat. He suggested Stefan leave before he tore his already bruised balls from his body.

Once I was back in the safety of my home, I sobbed uncontrollably in my mother's arms. My father paced the living room, muttering threats about any male that came near me. When asked to explain what had prompted the fight, I only said that Stefan had offered me a ride home and seemed to think that was an invitation to grope me. I never mentioned the insults or Ash. Despite everything I had gone through, I felt I needed to protect him. I asked my parents not to call the authorities, thinking it was unnecessary. It would be difficult enough to explain the black eyes and other physical injuries once he got back to the dance. Shifters heal quickly, but not instantaneously. I figured that would be punishment enough for him. I also foolishly expected to hear from Ash, to apologize or see if I was okay. The school year ended a week later, and I never heard from him.

I struggled internally to let go of those memories and return to the present, where Nico and a fully grown (and even hotter) Ash stared at me in shocked silence.

"Yeah, well, this has been nice," my roommate mumbled as he took my arm and pulled me deeper into the room. "Oh look, there's my mother. Better let her know we're here."

If we had been a cartoon, we would have left skid marks on the thick carpeting in Nico's rush to get us out of there.

CHAPTER 3

Once he had put enough people and a potted plant between us, Nico whispered, "What was that about? Why did you growl at him?"

"Growl? I did not growl at anyone. I was letting him know that I did not need his assistance."

"Tai, you literally growled. Like, bare your teeth at him and everything."

My BFF had not been at the prom. Vampire puberty had taken him from a pimply, angst-filled teen to a bloodsucking angst-filled teen in a matter of days. *Contrary to what popular fiction would tell you, Vampires are born, not made. Around age 16, they go through their own version of puberty. A genetic component in their endocrine system kicks in, and it becomes necessary for them to consume blood. This consumption comes with its drawbacks and benefits. First off, there was the whole sensitivity to sunlight thing. But they gained strength, speed, and an extended life span.* They usually seclude themselves during the transition, and he had missed out on all the "fun" that night. I also had seen no reason to share my humiliation with him.

"I promise to tell you all about it later. But not here and not now. I should call an Uber and head home. You stay and make nice with everybody, and I'll see you there."

Nico shook his head firmly. "Not going to happen. You're here and will deal with whatever caused that hissy fit. And yes, you also hissed at him. But you're right. We are going to talk later. Now follow me. I see my maternal parental unit near the buffet."

Trailing behind Nico, I tried to make myself as inconspicuous as possible. But my eyes were captured by the man speaking to his mother. He was tall by human and vampire standards. His black hair

16

curled at the base of his neck, where it met the collar of his white shirt. His crystal blue eyes met mine as I tried not to stare. On the one hand, he was a handsome man. But there was also something off-putting about him. Maybe it was the cruel twist I imagined I saw in his lips or the way his eyes seemed to dissect me like a lab animal.

Turning to see what her companion was staring at, Vanessa Rodrick (aka Mummy) held her hands out to Nico and drew him in. Brushing the barest of kisses on his cheeks, she stood back and looked him up and down with an appraising eye.

Turning to her companion, she said, "Viktor, I would like to introduce my son, Nicodemus. Nicodemus, Viktor owns this charming little club and has been gracious enough to offer it to the council for our meeting."

Wincing slightly at Vanessa's condescending tone, Viktor shook Nico's hand and immediately dropped it before turning to me. "And who is your delightful companion?"

Trying not to shrink away from his outstretched hand, I placed mine in it and schooled my face not to show how much his touch unnerved me. "My name is Tai. I'm a friend of the family."

"Oh yes, Tai. She is a little friend that my son acquired in school." She made me sound like a freaking virus.

"Not so little to my eyes. You are quite lovely," he commented as I tried in vain to remove my hand from his grip politely. "Viktor Asmuth, at your service."

His appearance might say twenty-first-century hipster, but his language hinted at someone much older. Turning my hand, he exposed the inside of my wrist and stared intently at my bracelet.

"Such a charming piece. What is the significance of it?"

Finally reclaiming my hand, I secretly tried to wipe it on my dress. "No significance. Just a family piece my mother handed down to me."

That was as close to the truth as I was willing to share with this man. Frankly, I wasn't even comfortable sharing the same air with him.

"It is a fascinating piece. Would you consider letting me examine it closer? I am a connoisseur of jade, and its carving is unique."

"I'm afraid not. It belongs to my mother, who would be quite upset if anything happened to it." A lie, but a small one. I decided that was more diplomatic than saying what I was feeling.

"Just let the man look at it, Tai. He's not going to steal it." Nico's mother grabbed my wrist. I don't know who was more startled when a growl worked its way up my throat.

"Oh, I'm terribly sorry. Guess I'm hungrier than I thought. I bet people could hear my stomach growling across the room. Excuse me while I get something to eat." Not the smoothest excuse, just the first one that came to me. I turned and went down to the other end of the buffet and began filling a plate.

"I'm glad I am not the only one to elicit that response tonight," a familiar voice said as warm breath tickled my ear. I must have been hallucinating because I could have sworn he sniffed me.

Feeling trapped, I grabbed an appetizer and stuffed it in my mouth. No one could expect me to talk if my mouth was full. Now all I had to do was keep eating until I could leave.

With a drink in one hand and plate in another, my eyes scanned the room. Finding no graceful way to extract myself, I lay the dish on the table's edge with a sigh and looked Ash in the eye. "Just keep that hound dog on a leash, and we should be good."

"I'm sure he was kidding around. Remember what he was like in school?"

"Well, we aren't in school anymore, and I'll break more than his nose this time if he tries that again." Feeling as if I had made my point, I turned to leave. I'd had every intention of making a grand exit. But that was denied when a small whirlwind with huge dark eyes suddenly tackled me.

"My Tai!" Anika Montgomery exclaimed.

Anika was Ash's much-pampered younger sister. I was still in the care of the local pack when Anika was born, and I was fascinated. When my parents transferred me to Maxwell, we bonded again, and she followed me around like a puppy. Hero worship at its best. Even on my worst days, when I felt worthless and unloved, her fierce devotion to me always helped. It broke my heart when I distanced myself after graduation to let that friendship go. But I was determined to put as much of that world behind me as I could.

Stepping back, I took in puberty's transformation on my young friend. Where Ash was a perfect blend of his English and Hindu parentage, Anika was an exact clone of her Indian mother. Small in stature with a smooth complexion that mostly resembled my favorite latte, she was deceivingly sweet. But behind those dark brown eyes lurked the heart of an apex predator.

The senior Montgomerys, Robert and Sunitha, were close on her heels. Theirs had been a true love story. They met while working for Doctors Without Borders, and it was love at first sight. But when dengue struck Robert Montgomery, Sunitha felt she had no choice but to change the man or lose him forever. The thing with shifters, if they infect (or change) a human, that person becomes bonded to them forever. It is more permanent than any marriage I have ever seen. Thankfully, they became the couple everyone hated because they were so happy together. It was also fortunate that though they were both doctors, Sunitha was also a shaman. I spent many hours at their home as they poked, prodded, and generally studied me. Thankfully those times were also filled with joy, food, and laughter.

Enveloping me in a tight hug, Ash's mother rocked me back and forth. "My precious. I have missed you so much. Where have you been?"

"Avinash, why are you making my little Pyaar stand here like this? Take her coat and find us a table immediately. I want to sit and visit."

Bowing to the inevitable, I held my arms out and allowed Ash to take my coat. His stunned look at my revealing outfit nearly sent me into giggles. A woman does like to be noticed, for all the good reasons. And when that notice comes from someone who previously rejected them, let's say if karma were a real person, I'd kiss them right there.

I took Robert and Sunitha's hands as I spotted an empty table not far from us. Settling myself into a seat, I spent a pleasant half hour catching up. As any proud mother is prone to do, I had to listen to a never-ending stream of praise about her children. Anika was attending medical school and was so bright she should be the one teaching the courses (according to her mother). But for Ash, well, the sun rose and fell on their firstborn child. I smiled politely and nodded at the appropriate places as I covertly watched their son as he mingled with the guests. Anika sat to my right and slid a folded paper napkin to me. She wrote "he's still single" in a nearly illegible script.

I casually crumpled the paper, handed it to her, and leaned in to whisper. "You will be an amazing doctor based on your handwriting alone."

"Ah, Nico, what a pleasure to see you. How are you?" Robert stood and offered his hand as my roommate came up behind me.

"I'm doing well, Dr. Montgomery. I hope you don't mind, but I must steal Tai away from you."

His death grip on my elbow stalled any thought of objecting. But then again, I think I'd heard as much as I could take. If I stayed longer, I'd either start laughing or crying. The jury was still out on it.

Pulling me behind the same potted plant as before, Nico turned his back to the room. "By the way, thanks so much for leaving me alone with my mother, bestie."

"What was she going to do, bend you over her knee and spank you?"

"I'm serious, Tai. She wants me to come back to Chicago and stay with her."

"So? Maybe she's lonely." I couldn't understand what the big deal was.

"Have you noticed all the people here? It's not just a standard regional meeting. It looks like it is a full house," he pointed out.

I took a good look around the room. From my limited perspective, I could see what Nico meant. I made out several branches of the troll families, gnomes, and shifters. A will-o'-the-wisp hovered over the buffet table as a kelpie dripped into the herring.

Looking toward the front of the room, I saw his mother conversing with at least half a dozen other council members, mostly uptight-looking older men with a few mature women thrown in. No one I saw looked under the age of fifty. So being Supes, they were at least a few hundred years old. I started as an elven delegate headed to the table and took the center seat. This was not the small intimate cocktail party Nico made it out to be.

Our little tête-à-tête was interrupted as a waiter handed us each a flute of champagne. "From your host. He asks that you join him at his table. The meeting is about to begin."

I glared at Nico and whispered, "Meeting? I thought this was just a 'little cocktail party'?"

Nico gritted his teeth and nodded to the waiter. "Thank Mr. Asmuth and let him know we will be happy to join him. Just give us a moment."

He turned to me. "I just gave you the same information I was given. My mother never said anything about a meeting. I don't want to get mixed up in politics any more than you do. But we can't just leave. I'd never hear the end of it. Let's sit with Viktor, finish our drinks, and then we can make an excuse to leave."

I looked over Nico's shoulder to see Viktor Asmuth staring directly at me with a predatory gaze. Taking a sip of what tasted like costly champagne, I searched for the right words to graciously get me out of there. I let my roommate once again take my elbow. Only this time, it felt like he was leading me to my doom. Something in my gut was screaming at me to run, to hide, to get the hell away from that man.

Suddenly feeling very flushed and agitated, I pulled myself from his grip. Pouring the rest of my champagne into the potted plant, I searched for a discreet exit.

"You go ahead. I need some air. I'll be downstairs in the bar. I'm taking an Uber home if you're not down by ten." Leaving Nico slack-jawed, I turned on my heel (or wedge) and headed for the first Exit sign I saw.

This evening had just been too much for me. Seeing Ash again and having to deal with Stefan had been bad enough, but the way that Viktor created a primal need in me to run was too much. I suspected that I was on the edge of a panic attack.

Shivers ran up my spine, and it felt like someone was following me as I hurried down the stairs. But every time I looked over my shoulder, no one was there. Then instead of going into the bar area when I reached the ground floor, I hit an exit door that led me into a back alley.

The third strike came as I leaned over to catch my breath. Pain lanced through my right shoulder and brought me to my knees as darkness threatened to overtake me.

CHAPTER 4

I want to say that my two years of kickboxing training took over and I conquered my assailant when, in fact, my need for survival took over. I lurched to my feet to run away. Unfortunately, my head was still reeling from the blow I received, and I ended up stumbling into the brick wall of the building next to Verge. Pain lanced up my right side from the impact, and I slid down the wall and onto my butt. Thankfully, as it turned out, since a round piece of pipe slammed into the wall where my head had been.

As I sat hunched into myself, I felt a hand grasp my left wrist, lift me to my feet, and twist my arm. The pain it caused was indescribable, but through it all, I realized that the thief/mugger was trying to tear off my bracelet. True survival instinct took over, and I had a perfect shot to kick him right in the (uh-hum) private parts. That momentary distraction bought me enough time to stumble down the alley. I was almost to the sidewalk when my relief was cut short, and I felt a hand grasp the back of the dress and pull me back into the dark recesses I had just escaped. Using the same trick I had used on Stefan earlier, I took a step back, ground my foot into his (I really wished I'd worn the CFMs now), and swung my left hand around to grab his junk and twist. Neither seemed to faze him, and he shoved me to the ground before retaking a swing at my head.

I had a moment of clarity before something truly primal from deep within myself seemed to boil out of me. I don't know how else to describe it. One minute I was struggling to escape, and the next, I found myself against the brick wall I had just bounced off, with my attacker against the opposing wall. As he raised the pipe again and started toward me, I opened my mouth to scream as hard and loud as possible (I should have thought of that earlier). But instead of a noise meant to bring someone to help me, an object the size of a baseball appeared. Glowing in swirling colors of red, yellow, and white, it hovered in front of my eyes. Without conscious thought, I grabbed the orb with my hand and used all my remaining strength to hurl it at my adversary.

The orb struck him dead center in the chest. His eyes opened wide in shock as a cascade of light ran through his body. The next moment, it seemed as if a form detached itself and hovered just over him. What looked like a shadow, shaped like a dog's head, hung suspended for a moment before opening its mouth and howling. The sound that assaulted my ears brought me back to my knees. Unable to cover both of my ears since my right arm hung limp at my side, I tried to endure the sound and prayed that it would stop before my ears started to bleed.

Sudden light illuminated the alley as the exit door was flung open with such force that it bounced off the wall. Ash led the way as a crowd of people, including my cousins, spilled out.

Rushing to my side, Ash attempted to lift me to my feet by my arms until I screamed bloody murder, and he gently lowered me back to the pavement.

Nico, Viktor, and my cousins converged around the attacker as the rest of the Montgomerys congregated around me. I only heard the voices around me dimly, as if from a distance, until I could no longer ignore oblivion's siren call and passed out.

Searing pain woke me as someone took my injured right arm and tried to rip it from my body. Or at least that is how it felt to me. The whole time someone who smelled of warm cloves and ginger held me tight and whispered in my ear. I was in too much pain to comprehend the words, but they still soothed me until I let the darkness claim me.

The dream plagued my sleep. The same dream I'd had since childhood. The same and yet different. I'm walking toward a temple. The walls are white stucco with red lacquered trim. I pass under an arch and make my way to the entrance. I expect to see a rather sizeable snow-white fox curled around the form of a sleeping red fox. Only this time, the white fox stands over the red fox, grasping it by its neck as it struggles. Finally, the red fox relaxes, and the white one settles back down and curls around it. And for the first time, I notice that the white fox has multiple tails. Before I can count them, I drift into an uneasy sleep.

I panicked when I finally returned to my senses, though the room I woke in was not the least threatening. Light filtered through blinds that hung from large casement windows and illuminated the pale gray walls so that they gave off a calm and soothing glow. I turned my head to find Anika sleeping in an overstuffed chair on the other side of the room. I moved slowly and as quietly as possible to avoid disturbing her. But her eyes popped open, and she rushed to my side. "Don't move!"

Of course, I had to immediately leap to my feet and start jumping around and flailing my arms. "What! Where is it? What's on me?"

Surprisingly, Nico was the first to burst into the room, tripping over the detested wedges that someone had left scattered on the floor along with the rest of the evening's ensemble. The Montgomerys followed close behind. It suddenly dawned on me that I was performing a freestyle dance in nothing but the thong and strapless bra I had worn under my discarded dress.

Between one heartbeat and the next, I was back under the down comforter that adorned the bed. "Where am I? Would someone please tell me what is going on?"

"Anika, I thought we told you to come to get us as soon as Tai woke," her father scolded as her mother sat by my side and smoothed the hair from my forehead.

I'm sorry, Papa, Amma. I didn't want her to hurt herself, which must have startled her."

"Startled? You nearly gave me a friggin' heart attack." Leaning into her touch, I gave myself a minute to enjoy Mrs. Montgomery's soothing caress and to let my heart stop racing.

All too soon, she stood and motioned for everyone to leave the room as I sat there and tried to collect my thoughts. Shortly I became aware of the sounds of drawers being opened and shut. After a few moments, she placed a bundle of clothes in my lap.

"Go. There is a bathroom through the door on the right. These pants and shirts will be too big for you, but you can't wear that filthy dress. Put them on and then meet us in the kitchen. I'll get you something to eat." After one final hug, she left the room and quietly closed the door.

Once in the bathroom, I undressed and took stock of my various injuries. Strangely, the palm of my left hand hurt the worst though my right shoulder was stiff and sore, making it difficult to put it through the arm of the T-shirt I held. The T-shirt was long enough for modesty's sake—it was longer than the dress I'd been wearing. Stepping into a pair of sweatpants that were a foot too long on me and twice as big around, I noticed minimal discomfort until the fabric brushed up against my scrapped knees. The back of my head felt like a sledgehammer was trying to beat its way out. I nearly fainted once I looked in the mirror and saw my hair's tangled horror. Grabbing a nearby bar of soap, I took advantage of the large vessel sink and washed my face, dragging my wet hands gingerly through my hair and slicking it back off my face. Nico had put so much styling product into it the previous night that it had no trouble staying smoothed down. I turned to leave the room and nearly did a faceplant after tripping on the hem of the pants. Moving slower than I would have liked, I took them off and tossed them onto the bed as I passed it. Following the sound of muffled voices to a modern kitchen stocked with all stainless steel top-of-the-line appliances, I sat next to my BFF at the glass table in the center of the room. I wrapped my hands around the cup of coffee handed to me and took a moment to gather my thoughts.

"Can someone please tell me where I am and what happened?" I asked.

"You're in my condo. We thought it best to bring you here since it was so close to the nightclub." Ash moved with a quiet elegance as he entered through the front door.

Blushing, I looked down at the shirt I wore as it dawned on me that it must be one of his. That would explain why it was so long.

Pulling a chair around to join us at the table, he sat far too close for my comfort. "What can you tell me about the human that attacked you last night? What did he want from you?"

"Human? No way. That guy was way too fast to be human. And the way he threw me around, that's not possible." I shook my head in disbelief.

"Did he say anything? Make any threats?"

I was starting to get annoyed. "Nothing. The man never said a word. Why aren't you asking him these questions?"

"I can't ask him anything. He's dead."

CHAPTER 5

I sat in stunned silence as everyone else started to talk at once. Had I caused the death? I realize that this now-deceased person had been trying to injure or kill me. But the thought that I may have taken his life left me sick.

Ash held up a hand to silence the others, then gently took my hand in his. "I need you to go over everything that happened. Take your time, but don't leave anything out."

So I went through everything I could remember for the next twenty minutes. When I got to the part about the man trying to tear my bracelet off, I panicked until I saw it was still on my wrist.

"Have you ever manifested anything like the orb you described before?" he asked.

I shook my head in confusion. "I'm not sure exactly how it happened. Is that what killed this guy?"

Before he could answer my question, his mother came around the table. I had not realized I had been shaking my left hand until she took it in hers.

"What hurts you, Pyaar? Let me see." Turning my hand over, I saw that the scar on my palm was blazing red. I never really paid much attention to it, usually. It was something I'd always had and never seemed to interfere with my life until now. Now it burned like a thousand hot needles trying to force their way into my skin. Clenching my fist helped a bit, but I wanted a pitcher of ice where I could submerse it.

Ash leaned in to get a better look as his mother hustled out of the room, returning a moment later with a first-aid kit. Instead of the Band-Aids and ointments I expected to see, the kit contained vials of oils and bags of herbs. Selecting two small glass containers, she sprinkled the contents of one onto a wet paper towel, then instructed me to hold it to my forehead. Meanwhile, she began rubbing a few drops from the other into my palm. Almost instantly, I began to relax as the scent of lavender enveloped me. Soon the burning in my hand waned, and I wanted nothing so much as to go back to sleep. But common sense won, and I took a deep breath and centered myself.

One question seemed to eat at my brain. "How did you know I was in trouble?"

Nico and Ash exchanged a glance. "I decided you were right and grabbed our coats. I should have been right behind you. But I couldn't find you in the bar," my roommate explained.

Ash continued, "I was downstairs because the boys called in that the club's security cameras had all gone black."

It took me a minute to realize that he was referring to Dunker and Sunreaver. I might have let a hysterical giggle escape before blanking my face and waiting for him to finish.

"Thankfully, I ran into Nico. That's when we heard you scream. My parents and Anika had just gotten off the elevator and followed us out."

"Yes, Amma and Papa both had appointments this morning, and I had an early class," Anika chimed in. "So we decided to leave early, and when we saw Avinash running out, we rushed out to see what was happening. You were slumped against the far wall, and that human was lying not far from the door."

"You were groggy when we first found you and making no sense. You kept muttering about phantom dog heads, balls of light, and how bad your arm hurt. You had a dislocated shoulder, and Dr. Montgomery reset it. By that time, you passed out. Ash suggested we bring you here," my BFF explained.

I don't know. My head was starting to spin from hunger or mental overload. But just as suddenly as it started, my mind cleared. "What about Viktor Asmuth? How did he end up outside? I thought he came out with all of you."

"I presumed he must have come down with my family when he showed up."

Ash's parents looked at each other before shaking their heads. "He wasn't with us. I just thought he must have already been downstairs."

Nico also shook his head. "No. He was with my mother when I left. I suppose he could have taken the stairs, like Tai."

"We can come back to that. For now, I want to hear more about this ball of lightning. Go over what happened when it showed up one more time," Ash asked, bringing the focus back to me.

"As I said, I had just tried to twist his manhood into a knot, which did not affect him. Then suddenly, I was ten feet away. I opened my mouth to scream, and this thing just popped out. I don't know which of us was more surprised. I don't know why I grabbed it, but I did, and it didn't burn. In fact, it felt slightly cool to me. Then I threw it and hit him with it. He lit up like one of those cartoon characters that gets electrocuted, and you can see their skeleton."

Abruptly, it hit me. I turned to look at Nico. "How could you have heard me scream? I never actually made any noise."

"I didn't hear you. Ash is the one that said he heard you scream and took off running. I just followed behind." Nico confessed.

A look of bewilderment settled over Ash's features. "You must have and don't remember it. I know I heard you."

"Maybe that thing came out of the guy after he lit up," I suggested with a shudder.

"We didn't see anything other than you and that man," Mrs. Montgomery chimed in.

"You'd just taken a blow to the head, from what we could tell. It was probably just a hallucination."

I pulled my hand away and glared at Ash. "I sure didn't hallucinate the sound that thing made."

Nico placed his hand on my shoulder. "I think maybe you did. No one else heard anything."

I would have jumped to my feet and fled the room. I am still trying to figure out where to go, but I would have made it dramatic. Ash's warm callused hand on my arm stopped me. I saw his concerned gaze and tried to look away.

"Tai, it's only natural considering the beating you took. The dislocated shoulder wasn't the worst of your injuries. You also had a concussion. You may be a Supe, but you can still be hurt. And this is going to take a few days to heal."

The spell broke, and my head started to throb. "Damn it, I hope I can heal by Saturday because that's my next shift."

"I'm afraid not. You'll have to take a leave of absence until we get this thing cleared up and you've had a chance to heal," Ash announced as if he had any say in my life.

Shaking my head made the throbbing worse. "Not going to happen. We're shorthanded as it is. I can't call off."

His look was both stern and regretful. "Unfortunately, you don't have a choice. The council has decided that you will not return to work until we investigate this incident. We need to know how that man died and that you were not the cause. So until that time, you will need to confine yourself."

This time I did jump up. Shaking Ash's hand from my arm, I looked at everyone else gathered at the table. But no one would meet my gaze. "This is bullshit. The council has no authority over my life. Not now, not ever."

"In this case, they do, Tai. If you're starting to manifest powers that can kill someone, they must know that you control them. If not, you could jeopardize the humans you work with and the whole Supe community. Either you follow their mandate, or they will confine you themselves."

I could feel my blood pressure rising as I got angrier and angrier. Suddenly the scar on my left hand started to burn again. Clutching it to my chest, I stood there shaking, not knowing how to react. Anika was the first to run to me and enveloped me in a vanilla-scented hug. Next came Nico and then the Montgomerys.

Ash stood back, seemingly aloof, despite the concern I still saw in his eyes. "The council will convene at 9:00 a.m. Monday, and I'll drive you there. We should have some answers by then."

Gently breaking away from the pile of love I found myself in, I turned back to Ash. "I'm telling you, that guy couldn't have been human. I may not be the strongest person in this room, but I'm no

31

longer that little girl you knew. I'm not Null and Void anymore. I do have some Supe strength and speed. That guy threw me around like a rag doll." I could feel my blood pressure rising again, and I took a deep breath.

Grabbing his arm, I tried not to notice the steel length of muscle just under his skin. I did. And if the situation had not been so dire, I might have succeeded. "You must believe me. I'd have had no trouble getting away from him if he had been human."

His gaze seemed to linger on my face before he gave a curt nod. "I had some of my cameras set up around the perimeter of the building. They weren't affected by whatever took out the club's cameras. Let me go over them. See, what if they picked up anything."

I breathed a sigh of relief—too soon.

"Don't get your hopes up, though. They only covered a few key areas. But it can't hurt to look."

Mrs. Montgomery pressed a bowl of soup into my hands. "Drink. You need something in your stomach."

I took a long swallow of what tasted like a lemon-infused chicken broth and gazed out windows overlooking the lake. It took me a minute, but it dawned on me that the sun was setting. How long had I been asleep? I must have said that out loud because Ash instantly answered me.

"You have been out about eighteen hours."

My first concern was for Magoo. But my roommate seemed to anticipate my questions before I could even voice them.

"Fat boy's fine. I've been home and made sure he was fed. Not that he appreciated it," he said as he held out a hand decorated with rapidly healing cat scratches. They had a somewhat strained relationship. Okay, Magoo hated him and was not afraid to show it.

Relieved that my second favorite feline (don't judge me) was taken care of, I dropped back into my chair. "I still can't understand what's happening. I'm a Null. Nulls don't shoot fireballs out of their mouths."

I saw a look pass between the elder Montgomerys. The couple seemed to make some decision and sat back.

"Well, we have a theory about that," Robert Montgomery said as he laced his hands together and leaned toward me.

Sunitha expanded on that comment. "We think that perhaps your talents are somehow being suppressed. We don't know how or why."

"I don't understand. Why would you think that?"

"I think it has to do with your tail when you first came to the Alpha's house. I was only four then, but I remember that cute little red tail," Ash commented.

Was it cute or creepy that a preschool-age Ash had been checking me out? I was going to vote for cute because my self-esteem needed a boost right about then.

"Yes, he liked it so much he kept pulling on it. When it finally disappeared, we told him it was his fault for always tugging on it. The poor boy was in tears for days."

Embarrassed by the discussion, said boy cleared his throat and excused himself from the room.

"What do you mean it disappeared? How does a tail vanish?" I asked.

Robert picked up the conversation. "It was there for about a week after you came to us. The following day it was gone, with any indication that you were anything other than a regular toddler. Whatever is affecting you must have taken that long to completely take control. If you had been found at that time instead of a week earlier, you would have gone to a human foster home."

Shaking my head, I announced, "That's it. I'm done. I don't think I can deal with anything else right now. Nico, would you please take me home? I need time to process everything."

Ash reappeared, carrying my coat, a pair of women's leggings, and my shoes. I did not want to think about why he had ladies' clothing in his condo—none of my business.

"I'll take you home. I want to go over a couple of things with you."

Desperate to put some distance between us, I sent a pleading glance to my BFF.

"That would be great. I'm due at the club in an hour, and if I'm late, I won't be able to get my makeup right." He must have spilled the beans about his hobby because nobody blinked an eye—dirty, rotten bastard.

CHAPTER 6

A short time later, I found myself tucked into the passenger seat of Ash's Tesla sans pants because ick. I wasn't wearing some unknown skank's coochy-hugging pants. Instead, I buttoned my coat from chin to knee, put my wedges on, and marched out the door. But only after getting a round of hugs dished out with instructions from the doctors Montgomery and a doggie bag with soup and chapati bread inside.

I kept quiet (I know, right?) until Ash had navigated through downtown traffic and we were cruising along the highway. I spent that time surreptitiously studying his profile. Dark gold hair curled just over the collar of his shirt. His nose might be broader than was fashionable, but I found it suited his face. In profile, his long eyelashes matched the color of his hair—a perfect complement to his golden eyes.

I averted my eyes before he could catch me. I know I owed him for last night. But I had a hard time articulating it. Plus, I was feeling reticent.

Finally, I said, "Thank you."

He took his eyes off the road for a moment as he glanced at me. "What for?"

"For giving up your bed and home last night to take care of me. It must have been rather crowded with everyone there."

With a faint shrug, he answered, "I guess my mother didn't give you the grand tour. I have three bedrooms. My family uses it as a second home. Those were Anika's pants that I brought out for you."

I was stupidly happy to learn that the pants I rejected (I must remember to apologize to his sister) had not belonged to some floozy of his.

"Still, most people would have just called an ambulance and been done with it."

"I don't know what type of friends you have now. But you never leave one of your own. At least, I don't."

A shiver of pleasure ran up my spine.

Then he had to ruin it. "Besides, explaining how quickly you were healing to a human doctor would be hard."

Being a Null was like having the worst of both worlds. Other Nulls are the only friends you can relate to. Supes look down on us, and we can never fit entirely into the human world. That made it hard for me to let anyone except Nico get close. Whenever they started getting too close, I'd usually sabotage them. I've had my share of dates, mainly with humans. But the relationships lasted only a few weeks.

I let out a heavy sigh. "Well, it was still nice of you to ensure I was taken care of."

The rest of our conversation consisted of me giving him directions, and we were pulling into my driveway too soon. He was at my door before I unbuckled myself. As we walked up to the house, I took a moment to search for my keys, though it was unnecessary. Light suddenly spilled from the front door. Next to me, I could feel Ash tense, partially shifting so that his hands were tipped with deadly claws.

"Why you stand out in the cold? Come in, come in," Uka called.

I put my hand on Ash's arm." You can relax. It's just my neighbor. She's like a grandmother to me."

"Your grandmotherly neighbor has a key to your house?" he whispered.

I just shrugged and led him up the drive.

Walking up to my porch, I introduced them to each other. "Uka, this is Avinash Montgomery, an old friend of mine."

She sniffed and leveled a disapproving stare at me. "Out playing with *neko* all night."

I could feel a flush running up my neck and hoped that Ash did not know Japanese. *Neko* was a word for "cat."

"It's not like that, Uka."

Ash stopped me before I could go on. "Tai was attacked last night, and my family and I took care of her."

For a moment, it almost seemed like a veil was lifted over Uka's face, and I got a glimpse of something foreign before it slipped back into place. Stumbling down the steps, she wrapped me in a floral cloud of perfume and rocked me.

"Chan, are you all right? Where are you hurt?" I learned that *chan* is a Japanese endearment. She often used it for me. Nico, she just called "him" or "you."

Dragging me into the house, she let the screen door swing close on Ash. Quick thinking kept his face from injury, but he was not as lucky with the front door itself. I heard a muffled "umph" and mumbled swearing as I was pulled into the kitchen.

"You sit. I make you something to eat, and then you go to bed."

"You don't need to do that, Mrs. Uka. My mother sent some soup home for Tai."

She speared him with a piercing glance before a mask of benevolence settled over her features. "No *missus*, just Uka."

Magoo took that moment to stroll into the kitchen. Ignoring me, he headed straight for Ash and wove between his legs, completely covering the bottom of his black dress pants in hair. Satisfied that his work was done, he finally seemed to notice my presence and stood on his back legs, clawing at my bare ones under the coat.

Peeling the cat from my legs, I tried to gauge the room's mood. Anxious to avoid any awkward observations, like the fact that I was wearing nothing but a T-shirt under my coat, I headed for my bedroom.

"I'm just going to put on some pants—I mean, change clothes. I'll be right back."

Dashing out of the room, I made it to my bedroom and hurriedly divested myself of the clove-scented shirt. Grabbing my favorite yoga pants and an old work shirt, I started to fold Ash's T-shirt to return it, but I had second thoughts. I didn't want to have to explain anything to Uka.

My entrance into the kitchen found Uka at the stove, reheating my food. Ash just stood, taking in his surroundings. Glancing around the kitchen, I tried to see it through his eyes. Having updated it the previous summer, it had become my favorite room in the house. The vinyl floor was designed to look like reclaimed wood, and a fake tin backsplash over the sink gave the room a country look. A pub-style table and stools provided an informal place to eat or work. It might not be the large modern kitchen that Ash had, but I loved the warmth of it, especially when I could smell the heavenly scent of homemade chicken soup.

Uka set a steaming bowl on the table and motioned me to sit. I let no time pass between hopping onto a stool and digging into it. Ripping off a piece of bread, I soaked up some of the lemony goodness and groaned as I put it in my mouth. Glancing up, I noticed Ash's eyes locked on my lips. Thinking I had dribbled a little, I took a moment to wipe my mouth.

"Sorry, guess I was hungry," I murmured.

Pushing away from the counter he had been leaning on, he cleared his throat and said, "You're in good hands, so I guess I'll be going. I'll pick you up at eight Monday morning for your interview. We can talk then."

I started to stand, but he motioned me to sit back down. "I can see myself out. Call me if you need anything." He turned and walked back the way we came.

Uka stood silent until we heard the front door close. "So you like Neko?"

"It's not like that. We're just old-school friends," I said as I felt my face turning red.

"Uka will believe that when you do."

I finished my meal under her careful stare. Despite the amount of sleep I had already gotten, the warm soup had me nodding at the table. Stumbling a bit, I gave Uka a warm hug and sent her home so I could go to bed. Any lingering questions I'd had for Ash would have to wait for Monday.

I woke as soon as I heard someone moving around the house. Peeling one eye open, I could see the predawn light as it tried to make its way through my curtains. Suspecting that it was Nico, I didn't bother trying to be stealthy. Stubbing my toe on the edge of the door, I let out a string of curse words that were silenced when I heard a menacing growl from Nico's room.

"Nico, is that you? What's going on?"

"Who're you talking to, Tai?" my roommate said from right behind me.

Covering my mouth to suppress a shriek, I turned on him. Slapping him with the back of my hand across his chest, I said, "Don't sneak up on me! What the hell is in your room?"

He looked puzzled until another growl issued through the door. Paling (which is a real trick for a vampire), he replied, "I just walked in."

The way this bungalow was set up, my bedroom was at the front of the house, with doors into the living room and hallway. Nico's room was in the back, with only one way in or out. Technically, it was the main bedroom. But I had let him have it since it had a much larger closet.

Considering the door was shut, I decided whatever was in there must have come in through the window overlooking the backyard. Moving as quietly as we could, we pressed our ears to the closed door just as an explosion of barks and hisses emanated. Panicking at the thought that Magoo had somehow gotten trapped in the room with some satanic creature, I burst through the door. What I saw next had me questioning my sanity. My twenty-pound senior cat, the same cat that couldn't be bothered when we had mice in the house, was beating the crap out of a dog. I'll call it a dog, though it looked more like a cross between a mastiff and a crocodile. It only took a moment for me to charge headlong into the fray. Wielding the walking stick Nico had propped by the door, I beat the hound across the head. Nico leaped over me in a display of athletics that I could not believe. Landing on the creature's back, he bit into its neck with the fangs that instantly descended into his mouth. Outnumbered and overwhelmed, the whatever-it-was collapsed to the floor, and a high-pitched howl, like the one I'd heard the other night, escaped its lips.

Covering my ears, I waited for the ear-piercing sound to dissipate before opening one eye. The scene before me would have been comical if we hadn't just fought off some monster in our home.

Nico's face had turned rather green as he bent over and tried to spit out whatever he had ingested. Meanwhile, Magoo sat quietly grooming himself as if nothing had happened. First his paws, then his face, then both of his tails.

Both of his tails? I wondered if the concussion I sustained the other night was playing with my head. But even Nico stopped his retching long enough to throw me a puzzled look.

"Am I seeing this right? Does Magoo have two tails?" he asked.

Before I could form a coherent answer, Uka burst through the back door. Stopping abruptly in the doorway, she raised her face and sniffed the air. I dragged Nico out of the room and slammed the door before she could see the carnage that the creature had wreaked.

"What have you been doing, foolish girl? Why is inugami hunting you?"

CHAPTER 7

We convinced Uka that the noises she heard were from a raccoon that had gotten in through the attic. Once she was gone, I spent the rest of the morning helping Nico clean up the mess that that thing had created. I also consoled him because losing a replica of the ruby slippers from his favorite movie "ruined his life," though I was "not funny" suggesting we paint a pair of sneakers with red paint. Surprisingly, there was nothing of the creature to clean up. The only evidence that it had ever been in the room was the torn screen on one window. Where or how it left was a mystery.

Once that was done, we looked up the meaning of *inugami*. Of course, first, we had to figure out the proper spelling. During this time, Nico repeatedly scolded me for not knowing more about my Japanese heritage. I responded by daring him to recite the alphabet in Welsh.

All bickering aside, neither of us was happy with what we found. According to an online encyclopedia, *inugami* was the name of a "dog spirit used as a familiar." I won't go into the gross details of how these poor spirits are made. Despite one trying to disembowel my cat (and presumably myself), I couldn't help but be horrified and depressed by the method used to create them. It hurt me to know what those innocent creatures went through.

Exhausted to the point of incoherency, I left Nico to finish putting fresh linens on his bed. Though he didn't sleep in a coffin, he was obsessed with black satin sheets. But it wasn't until I felt myself dozing off while running my hand down Magoo's back that I realized we had never addressed the two-tailed feature my cat now sported.

Deciding to save that issue for later, I let myself drift into a dreamless slumber.

After a few hours of sleep and a much-needed shower, imagine my surprise to find my BFF and Avinash Montgomery enjoying coffee and chatting like two old friends. Which they weren't. In school, they only had a nodding acquaintance, and that was because of me.

Wait, was I envious of Nico and Ash getting along? I was curious to know if I was jealous of Nico or Ash. Either way, I found that emotion unacceptable and pasted a pleasant smile on my face as I headed straight to the fresh pot of coffee calling my name. I took a fortifying sip before turning to look directly at them.

"To what do we owe the pleasure? I didn't think I'd see you again until tomorrow morning." Tomorrow was Monday, right? I hoped so; otherwise, my pronouncement would have made no sense.

Ash's gaze drilled into mine as he tightened his jaw. "Why didn't you call me?"

For a moment, I contemplated playing dumb. But I knew what Ash must be referring to, and since Nico refused to meet my eyes, I knew who the snitch was. "Well, in the first place, I'm a grown freaking woman, so don't talk to me like I'm a child. And in the second place, I don't have your number."

I turned to pull myself onto the kitchen counter since the only two seats were taken. Turning back to face both the men, I was startled to find Ash standing just a few inches away from me. Damn, he could move fast.

"I just looked up the number for Bagha Security and asked to have him paged," Nico provided.

Refusing to take my eyes off the man in front of me, I answered my friend, "Yes, and we will discuss why you did that later."

"Why? Because two attacks in as many days seemed strange to him, and he wants to keep you safe," Ash bit the words out.

I jumped off the counter, forcing Ash to back up or wear me. "As you can see, we have everything under control." If I say it enough, it might become real. "I'm fine. No worse for wear."

My traitor cat strutted in at that moment, and I swear he posed for us.

I tried to act calm as Ash crossed the room and squatted in front of Magoo. "No one thought it relevant to mention this development?"

Rolling my eyes, I hefted the cat into my arms and turned to shield him with my body.

"Tai, I am not going to hurt your cat. I want to figure out what is going on around here."

Ash took a deep breath before speaking again. "Please put him down, and let's discuss this. Please."

He turned and waved Nico out of his chair and motioned with his hand that I should sit. Setting Magoo on the floor, I watched him warily as I took a seat. Nico tried to take that opportunity to run away, but I pointed my finger at him. "You. You're not going anywhere. Stand over there."

Ash retook his seat across from me. "Why didn't you use that fireball thing last night?"

I just shook my head." Um…because I don't know how. I told you before, it just appeared the other night."

"Walk me through this. What did you feel when it manifested?"

"I had been scared but suddenly got angry," I answered.

"Weren't you angry last night?"

I closed my eyes and pictured the scene. "Not really. I was just scared that thing would hurt my cat."

I leaned over to tickle the feline under his chin. "But he put up the best fight of all of us. Didn't you, my little man?"

"What did you say your neighbor called it?" he asked.

Magoo started hissing and spitting, then turned to look at us both. "Inugami."

Nico was the first to break the stunned silence. "That's it. I'm out. I'll be in the basement if you need me." Making a motion toward us as if he was dusting off his hands, he turned and disappeared down the basement stairs.

Magoo acted as if he had not dropped a veritable bombshell on us and started scratching at one of the pantry doors. "Hungry," he said, thereby confirming that we weren't losing our minds and he was talking.

Turning, I saw Ash come up beside me. He and I continued to stare silently at the cat until he let out a howl that had me running to get his food dish filled. It was his "feed me now, or I poop in your bed" howl. I stood as he fell face-first into the container and started eating.

"I take it you didn't know he could talk." He sounded somewhat bemused.

"No," I said, staring down at the cat.

"And the tail?"

"Showed up last night after the fight. Or maybe during, I wasn't paying attention."

"Hmm." He pulled out his phone and stepped away.

I kept staring at my cat as he gorged on the premium grain-free food I always gave him. His usual vocals accompanied this—a combination of purr and growl. The sound was so familiar that I was nearly lulled into believing the last few minutes and been my imagination. A light touch on my shoulder broke the illusion.

"How old is he?" Ash asked as he held his phone against his shoulder.

It took me a moment to understand the question. "I guess Magoo is about eleven or twelve. Uka gave him to me ten years ago, and he was already grown."

I listened as he returned to his conversation, curious about who he was speaking with.

"That's right. She thinks the cat is around eleven or twelve years old. Size? About twenty pounds." He paused to listen to whoever was on the other end. "Well, besides his size and two tails, I'd say his most outstanding feature is his rather large round eyes."

He made some notes on a pad of paper I kept on the counter. "Also, see what you can find on something called an inugami and get back to me."

"Who was that?" I asked after he had hung up.

"One of my research people. No one can touch him when it comes to finding information online. And he's discreet. We must keep all of this between the three of us until we know more."

I looked down at Magoo, where he sat taking an after-meal bath. "Four, if you count him. Right, buddy?"

He glanced up briefly before resuming his grooming routine. "'Kay."

Ash looked at his watch before giving me a gentle shove toward my bedroom. "Go put on some shoes, and we'll get something to eat."

He continued to study my cat like a specimen under a microscope. I think I heard him mutter, "And possibly a drink or two."

Half an hour later, I sat across from him in one of my favorite bistro-style eateries. I started coming out of my daze with the help of a strong margarita and a plate of poutine. Ash opted for a craft beer and bratwurst. We both dove into our meals, and the silence between us was comfortable.

"So tell me about Uka."

Well, there went the comfort.

"Why do you need to know about her?" I asked.

On that, he put his brat down to start ticking reasons off. "Let's start with the fact that Uka called me a cat the first time she met me."

That comment had not gone over his head as I had hoped.

"Then she shows up at your house as you and Nico are being attacked and seems to know what the creature is without even seeing it. Let's remember the talking cat with two tails she gave you. Is that enough reason?"

"He didn't have two tails when she gave him to me."

Exasperated, Ash tossed his napkin on the table and leaned toward me. "I know you think humor is a good way to handle awkward situations, but this is not the time. Something odd is happening with the council, and now this is happening. I don't believe in coincidence. There must be a connection."

Nodding my head, I quietly agreed with him and took a sip from my second drink while I gathered my thoughts. "There's not much to tell. She moved in next door the summer between my junior and senior year of school. So yeah, almost ten years ago. That summer, I had a tough time, and she seemed to pick up on that."

Picking at the rest of my poutine, I gave myself a moment to put the events in order. "Nico was off on some visit to Wales with his mother, and I constantly fought with my parents about getting my own car. One day, Uka asked if I'd help her with some heavy lifting in her garden. I don't remember exactly what. But she paid me that first time, and I just fell into the habit of helping whenever she needed me. Of course, I had to be careful not to make it look too easy. I could lift a couple hundred pounds with little effort by that time."

Looking at the congealed remnants of my meal, I tossed the uneaten fry back onto the dish. "There was a rather mangy-looking cat that hung around Uka's house. One day, she brought it over. It looked like she had bathed and brushed it. She said she couldn't take care of it anymore. My parents weren't happy, but he seemed to attach himself to me immediately, and they eventually gave in."

I smiled at the memory. "Magoo was such a skinny thing and had these huge eyes. It almost made him look like an alien. Anyways, those eyes are why I named him Magoo. After a cartoon character my parents liked. He has been my best buddy ever since. Sleeps with me at night and follows me all around the house."

"Go on," Ash prompted when I let the silence grow between us.

Shaking my head, I finished my narrative. "Not much else to tell. I went away to college for a couple of years but decided it wasn't for me. I finally moved back and went on to get licensed as a paramedic. My parents moved to Florida around that time and left me the house. After that, she adopted me and is always coming and going. She has her own keys to the house, and I have a set of hers. In case of emergency."

He just shook his head. "On the surface, it all seems too normal. But I don't buy it. I'm going to have my guy do some more digging."

Eager to change the subject, I tried to be nonchalant when I asked, "What did you do after leaving school? College?"

Settling back and making himself more comfortable, he grimaced. "I went into the army. Special forces. Did you know there is an all-Supe regiment? I can't say it was the best time of my life, but it taught me a lot. After being discharged, I took a few courses and started my own security company. We work in the Supe and human sectors and some government work."

His phone rang before I could embarrass myself and ask more personal questions.

He quickly answered it, nodding and frowning as he listened to whoever was on the other end. "I'll be there shortly."

He threw money down on the table and extended a hand to help me. "I have to go. One of the council members was attacked tonight."

"What happened?

"I don't know yet. But it sounds like you won't need to worry about going in front of the council in the morning."

CHAPTER 8

After Ash had dropped me off, I wandered into the kitchen. I noticed that his cell and home numbers were on the paper he had been writing on. I programmed both into my cell phone and hung the note on the refrigerator for Nico. Having slept late and been used to odd hours, I worked off nervous energy by cleaning. Magoo was oblivious to the turmoil he had created and lay curled up on my pillows. Around 3:00 am, Nico stuck his head up from the basement as I was vacuuming under the stove. He just shook his head and went back to his computers.

Finally, I sat at the kitchen table with a mug of tea and waited for the sun to come up. I was still determining my exact plans, but I needed answers from Uka. Knowing she was an early riser, I estimated I had about an hour before marching next door. Pain lanced through my eyes, and I pushed the tea aside to rest my head on my arms. Just for a moment, just till the pain passed.

I nearly fell out of my chair when my phone alerted me to a text message a couple of hours later. Making my way across the kitchen, I took a couple of aspirin before looking at it.

> *Anika will pick you up at 3:00 p.m. and bring you
> to Bagha. Wear something loose fitting.*

No *please*, no *thank you*, no signature. Just something that felt like an order that had to be followed. If I hadn't already programmed Ash's number in the phone, I wouldn't have even known it was from him.

Tossing my phone aside, I grabbed a light jacket and headed next door. The house seemed quiet; all the drapes were closed, and no lights showed. I gently knocked on the kitchen door and waited. When I got no response, I jiggled the handle and was surprised to find the door unlocked.

Sticking my head into the door, I called out, "Uka, are you here?"

I stepped gingerly into the kitchen. Glancing around, the only thing I found odd was the silence. Usually, Uka would have soft music playing in the background from the old transistor radio on her counter. Unlike my updated kitchen, hers was the essence of the '70s, from its Formica counter to the avocado-green appliances. Dark wood cabinets fought to keep the room dark and feeling cramped. But it lost to the bright yellow floral wallpaper that covered all the other available wall space. A vintage kitchen set with red vinyl seats she took pride in was in the center of the room. It was the same table where I had spent many an hour drinking tea and listening to the older woman as she reminisced about life in Japan. I never did ask her what had brought her to Wisconsin, and she never offered any explanation.

Funny, now that I think about it. I had never ventured beyond this kitchen. A semiopaque curtain hung in the doorway, separating the rest of it from this room. I had never wanted to intrude, but suddenly I had an undeniable desire to explore the rest of the house. Reaching a shaking hand toward the curtain, I jumped back before touching it. It didn't seem right to infringe on Uka's privacy without talking to her first.

Leaving through the kitchen door, I circled her small yard and the garage that faced the alley. Peering into the windows, I was surprised to see an old dusty tarp draped over what I thought might have been a car. But I'd never seen her drive, only take taxis and, more recently, Uber.

Circling the property one last time, I gave up my search and headed back inside. Taking a chance that my parents might be home and not on the golf course, I video called them.

"What's the matter?" This was my mother's go-to response whenever I called outside our regular hours.

"Hello to you, too," I responded.

My dad's slightly oversized head suddenly appeared in the picture frame. "Hi, sweetheart. What your mother meant to say was 'what a pleasant surprise.'"

Smiling at his shenanigans, my mother pushed him over so she could also get in the frame. "I'm sorry, dear. Let's try that again. How are you? To what do we owe the pleasure?"

I took in my parents' happy tanned faces. Florida agreed with them. I had only visited them a couple of times, and on the few occasions they came back up north to visit, they were always anxious to get home. My father was born here and spent his thirty-year career with the MPD. My mother had been a stereotypical housewife and mother. Both were from hearty Germanic forest troll stock and had significantly mourned when they could not conceive. According to my mother, I came on the scene at the perfect time. She had given up hope of having a child, and when my father brought me home, she knew it was meant to be. It took three years of applications, interviews, and a broken arm before the local council decided that their home was the best place for me to be. None of us have ever regretted that decision. I could not have asked for more loving and accepting parents.

Suddenly very happy that I took the time to make an extra weekly call, I smiled at them before beginning my interrogation.

"I ran into the Montgomerys this weekend. They told me some fascinating information. Something that someone like a parent might have mentioned to me."

I waited, and when the only response I got was mirrored looks of confusion, I went on. "Daddy, you always told me you could sense the other about me when you found me."

He nodded once. "That's right, dear."

"So the fact I had a tail gave you no clue?"

"Well, how else would I have sensed it? It's not like there is a specific smell that distinguishes us." Obviously, he had forgotten the

50

distinct aroma that Sunreaver and Dunker had given off during their teen years.

"Oh, and don't forget those cute little pointed ears," my mother added.

I spit out the tea I had just sipped. "I had pointed ears?"

"Yes, cute little red furry ones. But they were gone by the next morning," she supplied.

"I don't suppose you took any pictures," I inquired.

"I think we may have one floating around of your tail." I heard a bit of a hitch in my mother's voice when she said that, and it hurt my heart. "But the ears disappeared so quickly we never got the chance. Then the Alpha took you away from us."

"Why all the questions, sweetheart?" my father asked.

Knowing I'd have to come up with an explanation, I decided the truth was the best route—at least part of the truth. I didn't need my parents rushing home, thinking I was in danger. I wasn't. I don't think.

"There was an incident the other night at the place they were holding the council meeting. Someone tried to mug me, and I might have thrown a fireball at them."

"See, I told you to move down here with us. That city is getting too dangerous. Oh, my poor baby. Are you hurt?" my mother wailed.

A rumble came from my dad. It was loud enough to be heard over the phone, and I reassured them the best I could before he went all alpha troll on me.

I kept as close to the truth as I could. "I dislocated my shoulder, but Mr. and Mrs. Montgomery took care of it, and I feel fine. Did they ever mention that I might not actually be a Null? They think that my real nature might be suppressed."

My mother shook her head. "They might have. But it didn't matter to us. You were our daughter. Null or not. You could have been human, and we wouldn't have cared."

What did I tell you? Best. Parents. Ever.

A knock at the door had me checking my watch. "That's probably Anika. I better run. Love you both."

My mom and dad told me they loved me while waving at me. "And say hi to the Montgomerys for us."

"I will," I promised as I walked through the house.

Opening the door, I was surprised when Anika pushed past me and looked me over.

"That won't do at all," she said.

I had no clue what she meant. "What won't do?"

"That outfit. Didn't Ash tell you to wear something loose?"

I looked down at the yoga pants and oversized T-shirt I had donned before calling my parents. "This is loose."

"Yes, and it is also completely shapeless."

Nico just happened to show up as she made this pronouncement.

"I know. This girl has no sense of style," he proclaimed as he grabbed my arm and dragged me to my bedroom.

Once again, I watched as my roommate went bottoms-up. Only this time, he was digging through my bottom dresser drawer. I caught Anika admiring the view before she blushed and turned away.

Finally, he shouted in victory and held a royal blue T-shirt aloft. He yanked the oversize shirt I had chosen (okay, it was one of my sleep shirts) over my head. Then he forced the way too-tight blue top into its place. I thank all the gods in heaven that I'd had the foresight to put on my one decent sports bra because the shirt he chose had a very deep V-neck that would have left nothing to the imagination. I instantly recognized it as one he had gifted me a few years earlier. "Cleverly Disguised as an Adult" was written in a fancy script across my chest and ensured that anyone we saw would be staring at my boobs.

Glancing down at my discount store athletic shoes, he sighed. "I guess this will just have to do."

"Why is it so important that I look good?" I was genuinely perplexed.

He got a bit of a smug smile on his face. "You didn't see how Ash ran when he heard you scream. Or the way he snarled at his father when they reset your shoulder. He even carried you the three blocks to his condo."

Anika covered her mouth and giggled. "I've never seen him like that before."

"I'm afraid your imaginations are running away with you. Ash thinks of me as a little sister."

In a singsong voice, Anika shook her head and sang, "Tai and Ash sitting in a tree, k-i-s-s-i-n-g."

"Enough!" I may have shouted that, but in my defense, this whole conversation brought up bad memories.

Both of my friends stared at me in shocked silence as I redressed myself in something more appropriate. I didn't go so far as to put my original T-shirt back on. But I did find a looser-fitting black shirt that didn't make my breasts want to pop out and yell "howdy." Then slipping on a headband to keep my hair off my face, I stormed out the front door.

I let the cool afternoon air finish settling my nerves. Next door, Uka nodded at me as she rolled a wheelbarrow up her sidewalk and into the backyard. Before I could chase after her, Anika came out and headed toward the small red car parked behind mine.

"I'm sorry, Tai. We were joking around," she told me as we buckled our seat belts. "I grabbed another shirt and some pants for you in case you wanted to change later. I think my parents are planning on taking us to dinner."

Giving her a half-hearted smile, I shook my head. "I'm sorry too. The last couple of days has got me on edge."

"My parents want to see what exactly you can do and find out if we can recreate the whole fireball thing. So Ash suggested we meet at Bagha and use their training room."

Oh, joy, I thought to myself as we journeyed to Bagha's offices.

Twenty minutes later, we arrived at an unassuming single-story brick building that sat on several acres of wooded land just north of downtown. The reception area afforded us a spectacular view of Lake Michigan. Still, it was the rest of the building that had me impressed.

Ash met us at the front desk and immediately led us to a bank of elevators hidden from view in what most people would assume was a conference room. He explained that the first floor was for use with their human clients and that Bagha conducted most of the business on the ones below. The lower ten levels housed everything from offices to a holding area for Supes who must be detained. Since human law enforcement did not have the capability (or knowledge in most cases) to handle Supes, they were brought to Bagha. There was even a dining hall that provided his employees' meals. Since many Supes had specialized diets, I imagined this must get expensive.

We finally reached the lowest level of the complex. We stepped into a hallway lined with windows, looking into what appeared to be exercise and training rooms. I saw men and women pumping an impressive amount of iron in one room. And in the next, about twenty people sat in a lecture hall, hunched over old-style desks taking notes.

I lost count of how many rooms we passed before arriving at a fortified door at the end of the hallway. After tapping a code into the pin-pad, the door whooshed open with a sound reminiscent of an old-style sci-fi show. Entering the room, I took a moment to survey my surroundings. Turning in a circle, I was blinded by the all-white décor. Everything was white, from the mats that lined the floor to the subway-style tiles on the walls.

I was brought back by Ash asking me if I'd had any formal self-defense training.

"Not really," I replied. "I take kickboxing classes, but that's about it."

Anika went to sit with her parents, whom I had just noticed, at one side of the room. Ash led me to the other side, where a row of punching bags hung from the ceiling by chains.

He handed me a pair of boxing gloves and pushed me toward one of the bags. "Let's see what you can do."

I assumed a basic fighting stance. Left foot in front and to the side of my right, I brought my hands up in the typical defensive pose. I skipped in toward the bag and gave it a gentle jab, accessing its mobility. Confident that it was sturdy enough to take a beating, I gave it a front kick and followed through with a hook kick. The bag swung freely, and I met its returning swing with a quick one-two punch and another hook kick. It was at that point I made a critical mistake. Hearing a woman's voice that I did not recognize,

I turned to see who had come into the room, forgetting one of the most basic principles of physics: *for every action, there is an equal and opposite reaction*. And that is when it hit me—literally. The returning trajectory of the bag blindsided me, and I ended up sprawled on the (thankfully) soft mats in front of everyone.

CHAPTER 9

Cool hands lifted me to my feet, and I came eye to eye with an intimidatingly gorgeous woman, taller than me, her thick golden hair was piled on top of her head in the messy bun I'd always wanted to do but couldn't. A boldly patterned sports bra and matching shorts showcased a lean and well-muscled body.

Next to her stood the elven delegate I had seen at the party. Topping Ash by a few inches, he had thin shoulders draped in a velvet cloak (can anyone say overkill). His long black hair was pulled into a high ponytail and anchored with an elaborate knot, while cold gray eyes showed no emotion as he stared at me.

She started laughing as she turned to Ash. "This is who the council thinks may be a menace to society?"

He just shook his head at me. "Rule number 1, never take your eye off your opponent. Try again."

I took up my stance and started from the beginning. This time I included blows from my elbows and knees. Each time I felt my energy level begin to wane, Ash would tell me to keep going. Through it all, I could hear her commenting on my moves.

"Really, Ash? The bag is hardly moving. Are you sure she's a Supe?"

"Look at that form. I don't think she could break through a paper bag."

"Please tell me she is one of the strays you like to take in."

Each comment dug a little deeper. But what put me over the edge was how blondie kept touching Ash as she spoke. The madder I got, the more furious my jabs and kicks became until finally, I gave a kick strong enough that my foot broke through the vinyl cover and

56

lodged in the bag itself. Don't worry, I never took my eyes off the bag. I have excellent peripheral vision.

Unfortunately, that did not relieve the pressure I could feel building up inside of me. While everyone else stared in amazement, I jerked my foot out of the bag, simultaneously delivering a blow with my fist that landed right on one of the seams. Sand and fabric burst from the rip I created.

Sweat ran down my face as I tossed the gloves aside. "I think we're done."

Stalking to the other side of the room, I wiped my face with the hem of my shirt. I gratefully accepted the ice water Anika handed me and finished it in one gulp.

"I don't think so, Ms. Jotun."

Ash grabbed my arm and squeezed it before I could open my mouth. "Tai, this is Melinda Paterson and Ailman Daecer. They are with the council and are tasked with evaluating you."

"Evaluate me for what?"

Blondie, aka Melinda, walked around me and eyed me up and down. Shrugging, she halted next to Ash and leaned into him. "Strength, temperament, and other things that could affect your Null status."

In Ash's defense, he looked uncomfortable with Melinda's proximity and slowly moved away. That didn't faze her as she reached over and laid her hand on his bicep.

"You must understand, Tai. May I call you Tai?"

She gave me no chance to say no.

"Your status as a Null comes with a certain autonomy that other Supes don't share. If that status changed, you would become subject to council rules. It's my job to observe and advise."

"Mel, may I call you Mel? Frankly, the council can take a flying leap off the Hoan bridge. Now excuse me, I have things to do." I turned to walk away and immediately ran into a mountain. Or at least it felt like one. Looking up, I saw that the solid chest I had run into belonged to Ailman Daecer. So much for a sensational exit.

"Before we continue our testing, I need to ask where you were around 10:00 p.m. last night," she continued as if I had never spoken.

Confusion clouded my face as I shot a look at Ash. "I don't see that it is any of your business."

"It is my business when one of the council members I am protecting is attacked. Most particularly, attacked with a fireball such as the one that killed your assailant."

To say I was surprised would be an understatement. I was also beyond pissed at Ash for not warning me. But I let myself relax, remembering I had the best of alibis.

"If you must know, I was having dinner with Ash. He dropped me off at my house around 11:00 p.m." The look on her face at that comment made the next two hours of "testing" almost worth it. Almost.

First came the treadmill test. A half hour of running at maximum speed and incline till I felt like my legs would fall off. Next came a series of strength tests, culminating with deadlifts. Five hundred pounds was my limit. That is not too bad for someone who generally eschews anything that might make them sweat.

Neither blondie nor the elf seemed impressed by my performance, informing me that the next series of tests would measure any residual magic I might have. Oh, joy.

"We'll be contacting you with the time and place. This is not optional, Ms. Jotun."

We weren't on a first-name basis anymore. What a shame.

I refused to move until Anika let me know they had left. Helping me to my feet, she led me to a locker room, where I took advantage of the showers. Thankful she had brought along fresh clothes. I winced as my muscles protested but got redressed before returning to the training room. I found all four Montgomerys waiting for me and did not object when they led me to the well-appointed cafeteria.

I lowered myself into a comfortable chair before saying anything. "Please tell me you have alcohol here."

Ash smiled at me as he waved down one of the kitchen staff. "Please have someone run up to my office and grab a bottle of wine from the mini fridge."

Not five minutes later, we all had a lovely glass of white wine in one hand and an array of food dishes that could feed an army in front of us. Filling my plate with a selection of battered and fried goodies, I could feel myself begin to relax. Imagine my surprise when Ash pushed his plate aside and took one of my hands in his.

"I am sorry about today. The council only notified me they would send an evaluator just before you arrived."

I just stared at him as I finished the mouthful of food I had just stuffed into it. "How did they even know that I'd be here today?"

He looked a little sheepish. "I might have mentioned last night that my parents wanted to evaluate how your abilities had developed since the last time they had seen you."

His father jumped in to defuse the conversation. It must have been evident from the daggers I was shooting from my eyes that I was not happy. "Tell us, son, what did happen last night? Who was attacked?"

Ash was more than happy to change the conversation by grasping the lifeline he had been thrown. "Liam O'Sullivan, about two blocks from the club."

"Where is he staying?" I asked. Suddenly as curious as everyone else.

"He has a room at the Pfister. Most of them are staying there since it is close. The others either keep apartments in town or stay on pack grounds."

The local pack had about one hundred acres just north of the city, where all types of shifters lived. It was where I had spent three years of my life, and I remember it fondly.

"What is he?" It would be rude of me to ask the person directly, but since he wasn't there, I let my curiosity get the best of me.

"He is a leprechaun from Dublin. Thankfully he was able to fight off his attacker. But he described a ball of fire, or maybe lightning was thrown at him."

"Did they catch the person who attacked him?" Anika wanted to know.

"No, and they want me to provide extra security. I guess they are expecting more representatives coming into town."

Mrs. Montgomery looked surprised. "I wonder why there are so many delegates here?"

One thing puzzled me. "Am I the only one who finds it strange that the elven councilman never spoke more than a couple of words today?"

"The elven kind are not known for being very verbose. In fact, they prefer to stick to their own kind. I'm surprised that one is even here," she added, then leaned over and grabbed my hand. "Let us do some of our own tests. See where your abilities lie and if we can discover what is releasing them."

I always had a hard time saying no to Mrs. Montgomery, so I nodded my head. "Just no treadmills."

I hope to learn to ask more questions one day before agreeing to anything. The best course of action was observing me through my daily routine while also performing simple physiological tests that they could compare to the ones I took in my youth. They were about to find out just how boring a life I led.

Bright and way too early the next day, Ash and his mother showed up on my doorstep.

I rubbed the sleep from my eyes as I leaned on the kitchen counter. "You know this won't work with all of you crowded in here every day. It's a small house."

Mrs. Montgomery just patted my shoulder. "I won't be staying. I am just going to put this heart monitor patch on you. We'd like you to wear it for at least two to three days. Short showers are okay, but no baths. You will also need to avoid microwaves, electric blankets, electric toothbrushes, electric razors, and metal detectors as they will cause interference with the signal."

Thankfully I had fallen into bed the previous night, still wearing the yoga pants and T-shirt I had worn to dinner. So while I did not present a fresh and clean appearance, I wasn't flashing anyone. I stood still as she pulled aside the neck of my shirt and applied a device right above my left breast. Once it was in place, we set up a time for me to go into their offices to review the results and do a few other exams.

"Avinash will help you through some simple endurance tests this morning. Now I have appointments to get to." Then giving me a quick kiss on the cheek, she left me standing alone with her son.

Clearing my throat, I asked if they had driven together.

"No, I brought my own car. I wanted to talk to you about some fascinating information, and I didn't want to bring it up in front of my mother since we are trying to keep things quiet," he replied.

"Can it wait until I get dressed?"

"I like this straight-out-of-bed, tousled look you have going on here."

I must still be dreaming because it sounded like he was flirting with me.

Thinking I was imagining things, I just shook my head. "Okaaay. Why don't I get myself together here? The coffee is in the pantry if you want to make a pot. I'll be right back."

Since I had showered the night before, I washed my face and combed my hair. Not knowing what type of tests he had in mind, I changed into a fresh pair of leggings and a simple long-sleeve cropped top.

Call me vain, but I did take the time to add a slight blush to my too-pale face and some mascara.

Magoo watched as I dressed, then jumped off the bed and followed me. "Pretty."

The compliment may have come from my cat, but I'd take it.

I experienced a sense of déjà vu when I returned to the kitchen and found Nico and Ash conversing at the table over steaming mugs of coffee. An empty cup sat next to the freshly brewed pot, and I helped myself to some after pouring my favorite creamer into it.

I accepted Nico's offer to take his chair, and he jumped up on the counter.

"I heard you guys talking up here and decided to nose in. What's up?"

Ash filled him on what he had missed, leaving out nothing. Including my humiliating face-plant in front of the council's evaluators. I'll have to remember to thank him for that (not).

"I think I might have discovered what Magoo is."

"You mean besides being my little goo-goo boy," I teased, leaning over to scratch my feline friend behind his ears.

Nico leaned over and pantomimed vomiting. "Oh, gag."

"No. From what my guy was able to dig up, it would appear that Magoo is what is known in Japanese mythology as a nekomata, or forked cat." He reached down and tickled Magoo under his chin. My cat or nekomata just soaked in the attention.

"Stories differ on many things. But one thing is for sure—they are yokai or supernatural beings. Legend says they can walk on two legs and eat human flesh."

"No," Magoo said. "Tuna."

Ash smiled. "And they are almost exclusively female."

We all looked down at him as he lifted his hind leg and went to town. It was evident to anyone who had the pleasure of witnessing this activity that Magoo was very much male.

"Some stories we found mention that when a nekomata matures, they slaughter their human family. In rare instances, they become the family's defender. I believe Magoo is the second kind."

Ash paused and looked me in the eye. "I want to know how your sweet little old neighbor came into possession of one."

CHAPTER 10

Ash decided we should start our day by visiting Uka, next door. But just like the previous day, she was nowhere to be found. I didn't want to remind him that I had a key to her house. That would be overstepping our friendship, and whatever answers she could give would wait.

We spent the remainder of the morning just walking or jogging and talking. Most of our walk took us along the lake shore to Kenosha and back. Over sixty miles round trip, done in less than five hours. I'd barely broken a sweat and felt invigorated by it all. I learned more about his company and the type of work they did. At the same time, I regaled him with stories of some of the more colorful patients I'd had to transport. He even took my hand at one point, helping me over a relatively large tree branch that had fallen across the path, then kept holding it as we finished our walk.

When we returned to the house, he opened the door for me and brushed a stray piece of hair out of my face. Feeling rather breathless, I invited him in and offered to make us lunch. But Ash begged off, saying he needed to make an appearance in the office, promising to check in with me later in the day. He left instructions to ignore the device I had taped to my chest. He also urged me to stay vigilant and not go out alone before leaving me standing in the doorway.

Feeling discombobulated from the morning, I made myself something my father used to refer to as a Dagwood sandwich, basically, anything from the fridge squeezed between two pieces of bread.

In this case, ham, pickles, cheese, lettuce, tomato, onion, and some chopped green pepper I had left over.

Eating over the sink, I looked down to see Magoo at my feet. His eyes were trained on my sandwich and followed its every more. Up to my mouth, bite, and lower toward the sink as I chewed.

Taking pity on him, I cut off a small sandwich section and placed it on a plate on the floor. He fell on it as if I hadn't fed him in days. It might be my imagination, but he looked like he was getting bigger. I needed to do some of my own research on the nekomata.

Wrapping the rest of the sandwich, I put it in the refrigerator and asked Magoo if he wanted to visit Uka.

He purred as he looked at me. "Uka."

I'd typically put a harness on him before taking him outside. But the look I got told me that would never happen again. I was confident that he could handle any stray dogs that might accost us, and out the back door we went.

I saw Uka in her garden the moment we stepped outside. Kneeling in the dirt, I could tell she was talking to the young plants as she put them into the ground. She always did. We made our way over there as quietly as possible but failed miserably.

"Why do you sneak, Taisetsuna? Do you need to talk to Uka?"

I lowered myself to the ground next to her. "Yes, I do. I have some questions. Did you know Magoo was not a normal cat when you gave him to me?"

She glanced at the cat by my side and got the biggest grin. "Yes. Uka is old, not stupid. There are many things that Uka knows."

Patting the dirt around the latest addition to her garden, she sat back and scrutinized me.

"Uka, is Magoo a nekomata? Is he going to massacre everyone?"

She let out a great big belly laugh at this. "Do you think Uka would gift anything that would hurt you?"

Leaning forward, she stroked my cheek with a hand twisted with arthritis and covered with wrinkles. And dirt. It was covered with lots of mud. "Uka would never do anything to hurt you, Taisetsuna. You are very precious to her."

I appreciated the sentiment, but it still did not answer my question. "But is he a nekomata?"

Smiling, she leaned over and stroked his back. "Yes, your friend here is nekomata."

"Is he going to get much bigger?"

She gave a gentle shrug. "Maybe. Maybe not. You ask him."

Glancing over, I informed him, "Much bigger, and you'll be sleeping on the floor."

He shook his head back and forth. "Bed."

I sighed. "I may have to get a bigger bed."

Uka seemed to delight in the back-and-forth between my talking cat and me. She took his transformation easier than I did, and I loved the big guy.

"So tell me about the inugami."

Her smile vanished in an instant. "The only thing to know is to stay away from them."

"That's a little difficult when they come crashing through your window."

She refused to answer, pressing her lips together until they nearly disappeared.

"How am I going to protect myself against them? I know nothing about them."

Finally relenting, she stood slowly and brushed the dirt from her knees. Then led me to her kitchen. "Come. Uka make tea, and we will talk."

I sat politely, waiting for her to make the tea. It always had a ceremonial feel when she made it. She would grind the tea to a fine powder and then add bottled water she had brought to a low boil. The tea was made in a clay pot that Uka calls a kyusu. Once it has had a minute to steep, she pours a little in my cup and then hers using a small device to strain out the ground leaves. She alternated this way until both cups are full. She then gifted Magoo with a small saucer of cream.

Waiting for her to sit at the table, I took a small sip. The warm fragrant liquid helped loosen the tension I had not realized I was carrying.

Uka sat staring into her cup, deep in thought, until I broke the silence. "Tell me about the inugami. How do you know that's what it was?"

She shook her head and continued to stare into her cup as if looking for a message. Finally, she pushed it away and looked at me. "Inugami are horrible creatures, created to serve one master. Many see them only as large dogs. It takes one with true sight to see its real image. You must be careful, for they can possess a weak person and use them to do their master's bidding. Once possessed, the person will die if the inugami is forced out of them. They cannot be killed, though. The only way to destroy them is to kill their master."

One comment caught my attention. "So these things can possess humans? What if one is forced out? Would you be able to see it?"

"Those with the sight will see a large dog's head, with glowing eyes."

Something was still bothering me, and it took a moment for me to put my finger on it. "But when you came in the other night, you never saw what was in the bedroom. How could you know it was an inugami?"

She tapped the side of her nose. "Wet dog and decay. Once you smell it, you will not forget."

Come to think of it, Nico's room had an unpleasant odor that night. We had opened the windows and turned on a fan to get rid of it.

The expression on Uka's face spoke of deep sorrow. I stood and walked around the table to hug her. "Thank you for sharing all of this with me."

She smiled sadly and patted my arm. "There are many things in this world that will seek to hurt or use you. Be vigilant, Taisetsuna."

I kissed her cheek and left her, staring into space. Her mind was a million miles away.

Later that evening, I sat with Nico and reviewed what Uka had told me. I was lucky he did not have to be at the club that night because I needed to talk things out.

"So I guess you weren't hallucinating in the alley," he said as we kicked back and enjoyed our beers in front of the TV.

"Nope, I must have driven it out of that poor human with my fireball. So I guess I have some responsibility for that poor man dying." This idea depressed me.

Nico came and sat next to me on the sofa, hugging me. "No, the person responsible is the asshat that sent that thing after you."

"We don't know that it was sent after me."

"Really? After one of those things breaks into the house, you still think you weren't the target."

Well, I was trying not to. The very thought of it made me sick to my stomach.

"But why would anyone be after me?"

"That's what we need to find out."

I was anxious to share what I had found out today. My phone suddenly rang, and I grabbed it without looking at the caller ID, hoping it was Ash. Much to my initial disappointment, it was Anika.

"Hey, Tai! Want to hang out tomorrow? I don't have any classes and thought we could get in some serious shopping."

I am never one to turn down a good shopping spree, so despite my initial reaction, I said I was looking forward to it.

Nico could read my face better than anyone I know. "If you want to talk to him, do it yourself."

I made an excellent attempt to pretend not to know what he was talking about and changed the subject in the only way I knew would work. "What is the new act?"

I found out over the years that one way to distract a narcissistic vampire was to start talking about their lives. Worked every time. For the next forty-five minutes, I was subjected to an in-depth analysis of his new show. It had something to do with Jackie O, but I wouldn't swear to it. His ramblings were better than any bedtime story.

For some reason, the day's weight suddenly hit me, and I wanted nothing more than a good night's sleep, so I gave him a quick peck on the cheek and made my excuses.

The next morning, I woke to the promise of a warmer-than-normal spring day. I wore shorts, combed my hair, and called it good.

At 9:00 a.m., Anika rang the doorbell, and we were off on a day of self-indulgence. She had scheduled each of us a mani-pedi, followed by facials and massages. While my expenses were relatively few, this was an indulgence that I wouldn't usually allow myself. But I decided to go for it. The last few days had been stressful, and I decided I deserved this.

The morning went by smoothly, except for the fight I got into with the nail technician. I had to argue with her to file my nails and paint them. I wanted to avoid long acrylic nails that I would have to repeatedly have redone. Besides, they would snap off my first night back at work.

The massage and facials felt like heaven, and I even splurged to get my makeup done and my hair styled. It turned out to be a waste of money. Nico could do a better job in half the time. But it was fun to be pampered for a change. Afterward, we decided to go to Verge for their lunch buffet. The day went to hell after that.

It was fun to watch a woman who could turn into a four-hundred-pound Bengal tiger pick at a small salad for lunch. I can personally attest to her ability to eat a whole family-size pizza (extra meat) alone, which was when she was twelve years old. I had no problems finishing a large plate of chicken wings by myself (no sauce as I didn't want to ruin my makeup). No matter my abilities, I had always had the Supe metabolism, thankfully, since I loved to cook (and eat).

The day would have been perfect if it had ended there, but before we could pay our bill and leave, Viktor Asmuth stopped at our table.

"I cannot leave two such lovely ladies to eat alone."

Mind you, we had already cleaned our plates. I mean, practically licked them clean. Then he insisted on treating us to dessert. Joining us for a decadent black forest cake, he was the perfect host. Too perfect. There was still something about him that put my teeth on edge.

Taking my hand, he looked deep into my eyes. "How are you after your horrible experience the other night?"

I gently removed my hand from his. "It shook me up initially, but I'm fine now."

He stared straight into my eyes as if trying to read my mind. It was starting to creep me out. Looking for a way out, I said the first thing that came to mind.

"Please excuse me. I need to use the ladies' room."

I hated abandoning Anika, but Viktor showed very little interest in her. Plus, they were in the middle of a lunch crowd. I thought she would be safe for the five minutes it would take to pull myself together.

Heading in the general direction of the bathrooms, I spied Ash coming out of a door marked "Office." Just as I started to alter my course to intercept him, Melinda Paterson followed him out, appearing less than put together. As I looked closer, I could see that Ash's hair was mussed up, and the tie he sported was askew. I could feel my blood pressure rising while my heart sank to my feet. I turned to make a discreet exit but failed.

I really had to work on that.

"Ms. Jotun. How fortunate to see you here." Blondie approached me with a smug smile curving her lips. "We were talking about you. Weren't we, Avinash?"

Ash stood silent and let her dominate what I hoped would be a short conversation.

"You're to appear before the council Saturday at 8:00 p.m. Please be on time."

She placed her hand on Ash's arm and squeezed it. "I'll see you later."

She strolled into the dwindling crowd with one final gleeful look at me.

CHAPTER 11

I was such an idiot. I just stood there, grinding my teeth. Finally, I managed to move my feet in Anika's direction. Dealing with Viktor was preferable to being here.

Ash tried to grab my arm, but I avoided contact with him.

"Tai, wait. We need to talk."

I turned on him, giving him the coldest look I could muster. "We have nothing to talk about."

I felt blessed when a person wearing the Bagha uniform intercepted Ash. I made it to the table, where I found Anika by herself (thankfully). Grabbing her hand, I dragged her out of the club and back into the bright spring sunshine.

We immersed ourselves in shopping for the rest of the afternoon. I ignored the constant ringing I could hear emanating from my purse. After the first couple of times checking it and seeing that it was Ash, I assigned him his own ringtone. Elvis's "Hound Dog." Seemed appropriate.

After hours of shopping (I think my credit card was smoking), we returned to the house. Nico had left a note suggesting we come to the club that evening. It was a better alternative to my sitting around and moping. So squeezing myself into the little white dress I had bought, I paired it with a short denim jacket to cover the monitor on my chest. Forcing my feet into a pair of real heels (there's a first time for everything), we made our way to Paisley Pete's to see Nico shake his stuff.

I had to close Anika's mouth physically once we stepped into the bar. It had a look reminiscent of an old-style nightclub. Round linen-draped tables were scattered around the darkened room. A tiny baby grand piano set off to the side of the draped stage. Once a week, the bar hosted a "torch" night, with husky-voiced singers lamenting broken hearts and lost loves—all while perched on top of the piano. I might have graced the Steinway once or twice myself.

The wait staff were all dressed in vintage clothing and weaved their way around the crowded tables with a grace I could never match. I should have mentioned to Anika that everyone would be dressed as a female celebrity. And they were all men. Some with beards. It was terrific, and I've loved the place since the first time Nico brought me.

The "hotness" station (yes, that is what they called it) was staffed by a maître d'. The only "male" staff in sight. It was Tony's turn at the podium tonight, and I was subjected to a long hug before he led us to a table near the stage. A Jean Harlow look-alike gave us menus and took our drink orders within moments. Then a few minutes later, "Liza Minelli" set our drinks in front of us. My phone took that moment to start playing "Hound Dog." I immediately regretted switching from my everyday satchel bag to a clutch. Removing it, I turned off the ringer and set it aside. Then Anika's phone started ringing. She grabbed it and excused herself.

I stayed occupied by studying the new menu. The club specialized in more appetizer-style food. But it was their cocktail selection that always made me giggle. Maybe because Nico and I had spent a somewhat inebriated evening with his boyfriend and the club owner, Peter, coming up with names for the drinks. My favorite was a mix that they served only in the fall. It was a pumpkin-spiced white Russian that I had named the Peter Pumpkin Eater.

Anika came back to the table, shaking her head. "That was Avinash. He wanted to know if we were still together because you weren't answering your phone. He sounded worried."

"What did you tell him?"

"Just that we are having a girls' night out. Why didn't you answer his calls?"

"Honestly, I don't know. I caught your brother and that Melinda chick coming out of a back room at Verge when I got up to use the bathroom. It looked like they had been getting hot and heavy. It threw me off guard." I buried my nose in the menu and refused to look at her.

"Oh, gawd! Not again." She had a disgusted look on her face.

"What do you mean?"

"They were an item a couple of years ago. Until Ash caught her cheating with anything, and I mean *anything*, that wore pants. Seeing her with Stefan was the final straw. You know how thick those two have always been, and Stefan said she wouldn't leave him alone. He should have kicked them both to the curb.

It was nice to know that I was not the only one who disliked Stefan and told her so.

"You know Stefan started hitting on me when I was twelve years old?"

I was horrified. "Why didn't you tell your brother? Or your parents?"

"I tried. But my parents kept telling me that I was wrong. That Stefan was just being friendly."

I just shook my head. "Friendly, my ass. That guy is a creep. He always has been, and he always will be. Your brother needs to get his head out of his ass."

"The last straw was when he attempted to talk me into taking Stefan as my date to prom my senior year."

Bile rose in my throat, and my ears started to ring. I never realized how blind I had been. How could Ash try and pimp his sister out to that sleazeball? "What did you do?"

"Well, since Stefan was standing there, I kicked him in the shins and called him an untouchable before locking myself in my bedroom."

I thought that was the funniest thing I had heard in a long time. Or maybe I'd just been drinking my Whiskey Business too fast.

"Can anyone join this party?"

I looked up to find my BFF dressed like Cher. This sent Anika and me into another round of laughter till we nearly fell out of our seats.

He tried to ignore us, dropping into an unoccupied chair next to me.

"These heels are killing me," he whined as he kicked off one shoe and rubbed his foot.

"Ooh. Big mistake, my friend. Never take the shoes off. It would be best if you toughed your way through it. Now your foot will swell, and it will hurt even worse," Anika advised.

"Well, shit," he said as he stuffed his already swelling foot back into the shoe.

A six-foot-tall bearded Shirley Temple came up behind him. "You're on next, sweetie."

Nico let out a long-suffering sigh and limped his way backstage.

While we waited for him to make his grand entrance, Anika and I ordered enough food to feed a small army. Or two very hungry Supes. Same difference.

The night passed in a haze of food, alcohol, and laughter. It was the best night out I'd had in a very long time. Nico killed it with his rendition of "Gypsies, Tramps, and Thieves." I even managed to coax Anika on stage with me for some karaoke after the shows were done.

Peter himself even stopped by our table. He was a little on the short side, but he made up for what he lacked in height in muscle. His medium brown hair was cut short enough that you could almost see his scalp, and dark brown eyes peered at us through tortoise-shell-framed glasses. Not my type, but I could see why Nico was attracted to him.

By this time, I had downed serval glasses of the Whiskey Business drinks and was working on finishing my third Rum-Rum-Tuger.

"How would you like to sing some songs in our next show?" he asked, resting an arm against my shoulder and playing with my hair.

I leaned in and stage-whispered. "But I don't have a penis. How can I work here?"

He just winked at me. "I won't tell if you don't."

This sent Anika into gales of laughter, and we decided to call it a night. Hugging Peter, I made him promise to have Nico home at a decent hour, and we stumbled out to the car.

Thankfully Anika drove since I'd consumed enough booze that I was staggering. With the Supe metabolism, that took a lot of alcohol. But I also had on high heels and would have done the same if I hadn't been drinking all night.

I sobered up quickly once we got to the parking lot and found Ash leaning against the car. The frown on his face was enough to almost bring me back to my senses.

"Did you ladies have a good evening?"

Anika, oblivious to the tension that filled the space between us, skipped over to him. "It was amazing. You should have come inside. Nico was awesome."

"That's great," he replied, never taking his eyes off mine.

I tried to straighten up and walk a straight line. But I managed to step on a pebble the size of a pea and tripped straight into Ash's arms. Attempting to regain dignity, I pulled myself away and straightened my clothes.

"Thank you," I said as politely and clearly as possible. But it came out more like "Th-th-ank you," followed by a burp and maybe a giggle.

Putting his arm around my waist to hold me steady, Ash wished Anika good night and told her he would get me home. It must have finally dawned on her that he was not a happy camper because she waved goodbye and peeled rubber out of the parking lot.

I let him help me into his car and buckle my seat belt. My brain fog was starting to clear enough that I was beginning to regret my evening's beverage choices, and I turned to thank him again. Only the look on his face had me shrinking in my seat. Before he came to a complete stop in my driveway, I opened my door to make a run for it. I could tell I still had some sobering up to do when I tried to exit the car with my seat belt still on.

"Hold up there, Princess Graceful." Strong hands helped disentangle me from the belt and lifted me out of the car.

After watching me wobble on my heels like a newborn calf, he scooped me up in his arms and carried me into the house. Kicking off my shoes, I leaned into the embrace. This would have been so romantic if he hadn't dumped me in the tub and turned a cold shower on me.

"I'll go make some hot coffee. Meet me in the kitchen when you get your shit together."

As I burst into tears, I realized why I never drank to excess. I was a maudlin drunk, and the last few days had been stressful. I sat with my head on my knees, shaking under the cold spray, and cried until nothing was left in me. Then I just sat, moving just enough to turn off the shower.

I must have dozed off because I did not hear Ash come back into the bathroom. But suddenly, Ash lifted me to my feet. Grabbing the nearest towel, he dried my hair and wiped my face.

"Can you get out of these wet clothes on your own, or do you need help?" he asked in a surprisingly gentle voice.

By this time, I was aware enough to assure him that I could change clothes on my own. I only wobbled a little as I went into the bedroom and pulled on a pair of jeans and a warm fleece top. Taking time to comb through my hair, I checked to ensure I did not have makeup running down my face. But the shower must have washed it all away.

I entered the kitchen and found a steaming hot mug of coffee waiting for me at the table. Ash had thought to put the creamer I liked into it. Sitting on the opposite side of the table, he leaned down and rubbed Magoo's ears. I quietly climbed onto my stool and let the coffee cool before taking my first taste. Damn it; it was perfect.

"What part of 'stay vigilant' did you not understand?" His voice was much quieter than I was anticipating.

"I hadn't planned on drinking that much. But I guess the stress just caught up with me. I just wanted to pretend everything was normal, that my life wasn't turning upside down."

He shook his head. "Burying your head in the sand is a good way to get yourself killed. I want to show you something. I had extra cameras set up around the club's perimeter the night you were attacked. They didn't pick up a lot, but what they got tells me a great deal."

Coming around to my side of the table, he leaned in and angled his phone so I could see the screen. The video began with a dark figure stumbling into the frame. If I had my bearings right, the person was across the street from Verge and appeared even drunker than I had just been. The figure unexpectedly stopped and appeared to be convulsing. He suddenly straightened up and headed to the alley where I was accosted. The time stamp on the video showed it was about five minutes before I came out the door. His gait was purposeful, and he no longer showed any impairment. That was where the video stopped.

Ash put his phone back into his pocket. "I have someone working on enhancing this video and some images from another camera. I should have those tomorrow."

He resumed his seat. "If you want to go to bed, I'll wait for Nico to get home. I don't want you alone until we figure out what is happening."

I wanted to fight, to argue that I could take care of myself. But I was feeling very lost and vulnerable. Maybe it was the booze I'd had or just fear of the unknown. But I did not want to appear weak. So I nodded as if I could see the wisdom in his words. At the same time, I wanted him to go. Preferably far enough away that I couldn't smell him. His scent was driving me crazy. The smell of clove and spices tickled my senses. It was both intoxicating and soothing at the same time.

I decided to redirect the conversation and fill him in on everything I had learned from Uka about the inugami.

He nodded his head as I spoke. "I had read about some of that but thought it was just stories."

I shook my head. "Nope. From what Uka told me, they are very much real, and the only way to kill them is to kill their master."

"I don't suppose she told you how she came to know all this information."

Again, I just shook my head. "I am beginning to think you're right. There is more to Uka than meets the eye. But I do know one thing—she would never do anything to hurt me."

It was all I could do to keep a yawn from splitting my face. I felt like I could sleep for a year.

"Go to bed. I'll wait here for Nico."

"You don't have to stay. Nico should be home soon, and until then, I've got my big guy here to take care of me." I leaned over and gave Magoo a good scratch as I said it.

"Much as I like him, I don't think a two-tailed cat is any defense against an inugami."

Magoo stood on his hind legs and hissed at that. "Protect." Then he rubbed against my legs. "Mine."

CHAPTER 12

It wasn't long before Nico came through the back door, singing and twirling around. He had changed back into his street clothes but retained most of the makeup he'd put on for the show.

Smiling in our direction, he came over and kissed me on the cheek. "I loved seeing you at the club tonight. How did Anika like it?" Not bothering to wait for an answer, he spun back toward the nearly empty coffeepot and poured himself a cup.

"You really should have come along, Ash. I was magnificent tonight. Peter told me so himself. He wants to take me away to Europe this summer, and I may go."

Ash gave him an icy stare. "I saw all I needed to."

"Ooh, it's tres chilly in here. Did I interrupt something? Should I go out and knock before coming back in?"

Ash got off the barstool and stepped over to him, backing my BFF into a corner. "And just where were you while Tai was getting so drunk, she could hardly walk?"

Nico raised one eyebrow. "I was doing the job I love to do. I was not hanging around counting drinks. I am not her keeper."

Ash moved even closer, getting right up into his face. "Well, as of right now, you are. Tai is not to be left alone until we figure out what is happening. And since I cannot be here twenty-four hours a day, you will need to pick up the slack."

I could see Ash's cat looking out through his eyes, and I heard the beginnings of a growl in his chest. I was all at once terrified for Nico and turned on.

My friend was still in the throes of a postperformance high. He did not realize that he was about to be nose to nose with a six-hun-

78

dred-pound tiger. It had been many years since I had seen Ash shift. But even as a youth, his beast was magnificent.

All traces of humor left Nico's face. "Do you really think she's being targeted?"

"I do. Just call it a gut feeling." Ash backed away as he calmed his tiger.

Walking him to the front door, I nodded and agreed to everything he said. Frankly, I was starting to get scared and wasn't sure I'd even be able to sleep.

Before leaving, he pressed his forehead to mine. "I have some people I want to talk to, and we need to see what is on those other tapes. I'll check in with you and pick you up Saturday to meet with the council. In the meantime, be careful. That means no alcohol, no sleep aids, and no cold medicines. You have to stay alert."

Nico snuck up behind me two minutes after he walked out the door. "So are things heating up with you two?" So much for being alert.

"Honestly, Nico, I don't know what the eff is going on."

Collapsing on the sofa, I filled him in on my day. Forget catching Ash and Melinda in flagrante delicto, the part that interested him the most was the new clothes. So I stopped midstory and took him to my room for an impromptu fashion show. After he approved every purchase except for two, I finished the story. He nearly fainted when he heard I'd been dumped in a cold shower. But before I could thank him for caring, he ran to the pile of wet clothes on my floor. He carefully hung up the denim jacket and gently spread the dress on the kitchen counter.

"Oh, thank God. We'll let the dress dry overnight, and then I'll use a cool iron. It should be good as new." He sighed in relief.

"Hey!" I pouted.

"Oh, give it a rest. You're fine. But this dress! Girl, you looked like a million bucks." Then he turned around and slapped my arm. "How dare you go shopping without me!"

I laughed and hugged him. "You were there with me in spirit. See, I used everything you have taught me about fashion."

He held up one of the rejected dresses—a very busy floral print with ruffles. "Well, except for a few exceptions, you did well. But this...this thing! This gets returned tomorrow, and if they don't take it back, I'll build a bonfire in the middle of the store and burn it!"

As luck would have it, it was unnecessary to build that bonfire. Thankfully it was very overcast the next day, so with a layer of SPF 50, Nico could keep his promise to Ash, and I could get out of the house. The salesperson I returned the dress to had the same visceral reaction to it that Nico had. Holding it by the tips of two fingers, she dumped it in a box behind the register with a shudder.

The next few days flew by. Not. I was able to spend some time outside with Uka. She had brought over more Saint George sword plants like the one outside my front door. Planting some under each window and near the back door, she assured me that anything evil would have trouble getting in. But in reality, the only thing that made it tolerable was wine (just a little) and Netflix.

Before I knew it, it was Saturday. I say that with great sarcasm since it felt like it should have been the Fourth of July already. I felt sorry for Nico, as he'd had to turn down a couple of shows to stay with me. I finally convinced him to do an early show on Saturday and promised not to step foot out of the house until Ash picked me up.

But Ash called while Nico was out to ask him to bring me to the meeting. He was still working on the other images that Bagha's cameras had caught the night I was attacked. I knew he worked long, hard hours to solve the puzzle. I made an excuse and told him that Nico was in the shower and made plans of my own. Throwing caution to the wind, I decided to meet Nico at the club. Even if I got ahold of him now, he'd have to change back into his street clothes and wash off all his makeup, and there would be no time to come and get me. So I left a message with Peter to have Nico wait for me. I planned to swing by and pick him up. That way, I'd keep my promise to be safe and have someone with me. But it also meant being alone on the drive to the club, but it was only a ten-minute ride; what could happen?

It felt good to be behind the wheel of my X90 again. As old as it was, I loved this car. It looked a bit like a small pickup truck with the bed cut off and a trunk slapped on in its place. With only two seats, it wouldn't have been practical if I needed to haul something. But it was sporty and came with four-wheel drive. Nico turned his nose up at it. Sure, it was a rather odd-looking shade of purple. But it was the first car I had ever bought, and I had a soft spot for the old lady (I called her Priscilla).

Pulling out of the driveway made me feel like I had won my independence. Turning north onto KK Avenue, I headed through the heart of my Bayview neighborhood. The cafes and clubs along the route were busy, and traffic was heavy. I blame that on not noticing the black SUV that was riding my bumper the whole way. I accelerated through a yellow light, hoping to lose them. But they ran through as it turned red and nearly took out a group of pedestrians in the intersection. My hands began to shake as I sped up, going at least twenty miles over the speed limit. Even then, the SUV was so close behind me that I could barely see its headlights. Unfortunately, the car windows were so deeply tinted I couldn't get a glimpse of the driver. If I could make it over the bridge, I'd be in sight of the club. Being a Saturday night, I knew they would have bouncers out front. Counting on the element of surprise, I poised my finger over the turbo button that was standard equipment when Suzuki made this car. Say what you will, but it could fly like the wind on turbo and turn on a dime. So as soon as we crested the top of the bridge and I saw the club's lights, I hit that button and pulled two car lengths away before they realized what was happening. I almost made it, too. But as I cut the wheel into the lot at Paisley Pete's, they managed to clip my back end, and the car began rolling. I hit the retaining wall surrounding the parking lot, and I know I hit at least two vehicles before the X90 came to rest on its side. Thankfully the only actual injury I got was when I fell trying to climb out the passenger window.

I was wearing flats this time, so I could only attribute my wobbly legs to nerves. I thought I saw double when two plus-sized Madonnas came running to my assistance. Then I realized one dressed as the Material Girl and the other a Voguing and Ball Culture Madonna.

The club completely emptied out as if that sight was not surreal enough. I couldn't believe my eyes when I saw Marilyn Monroe elbow Scarlett Johannsen out of the way, until I realized it was my BFF headed straight for me, followed closely by Peter.

Nico started to pat me down as soon as he reached me while Peter checked my eyes and had me recite the alphabet backward. I was still trying to figure out what that was supposed to do since I couldn't have done it even if I hadn't just been tossed around in my car like a pinball. Over all their fussing, I could hear the Madonnas.

"We saw the whole thing. That maniac just rammed right into her and took off," said the Material Girl, or maybe it was the other one. I was still a little rattled.

My head was beginning to clear when multiple police cruisers appeared, along with paramedics. With only a vague description of the style of vehicle and the direction they had gone, one unit took off with lights and sirens. At the same time, another officer relayed all the known facts over the radio. Even though I worked for a private ambulance firm, we had frequent interactions and contact with the city's first responders, so I was treated like one of their own. I sat on the curb while the medics took my blood pressure, checked my eyes, and did as much of an exam as they could. I waved off their attempts to get me to the hospital and watched as the parking lot became one big party. I just sat, stared sadly at my poor wrecked car, and winced when the tow truck pulled it away. Thankfully, the other vehicles I had hit were still drivable, and the owners were more concerned for me than for the repairs. Of course, having excellent insurance helped ease their minds.

It wasn't long before I sensed someone come up behind me. As I looked up, Ash sat down and put an arm around my shoulders. "I should be furious at you for lying about Nico being home. But I'm just glad you're not hurt."

"If it makes you feel any better, I'll be furious for both of us. I loved that car." I laid my head on his shoulder, holding my smashed phone out to show him. "And I was pretty fond of this too."

"Did you get everything you needed out of the car before they towed it?"

"Just my purse and this," I said as I handed him a slightly twisted piece of plastic.

He held it up to the light to get a better look. "What is it?"

"My dashcam. When I realized what was happening, I pointed my camera at my back window."

He laughed as he put it in his pocket. Gently lifting me to my feet, he brushed me off and took stock of my appearance. "Good girl."

I gave him a slight grin as Nico and Peter strutted over to us. "Why don't you two come inside and sit down? You can get some food while I change. Then I can take Tai home."

"Food sounds great. But I'll see you both get home in one piece. I was able to put the council off until tomorrow night," Ash commented.

It took Nico nearly an hour to transform into the suave vampire he was. Of course, that probably could have been quicker if Peter hadn't been "helping" him.

Ash filled me in while we waited. "From what I've learned, the European and American councils are in an uproar. Some of their members have either disappeared or turned up dead. Every victim they've found has been completely drained of their life force. There is little more than a dried husk left. They hope to combine forces and catch whoever or whatever is causing this."

"But why just the American and Europeans? Shouldn't they include all the councils?" I asked. I knew at least three others were African, Asian, and Russian.

He shrugged. "As far as I know, the victims have all come from those two areas only. I expect to get a list of the missing and dead from Alpha Benton tomorrow. He asked for my help with it."

Alpha Benton was the local pack leader. An older but still strong wolf, he had held his territory for nearly fifty years. He also happened to be the council representative for the mid-US region and the man who took me into his care when I was first found.

As much as I wanted a drink, I decided not to push my luck and stuck with water. But I did indulge in some of the best chocolate lava cakes in the area. I swear it was better than sex. At least, I think it was. It had been a while. But the time finally came when Nico was ready to leave, and I had to restrain myself from licking the cake plate clean.

We took a circuitous way back to the house, with Nico trailing behind. I wasn't even paying attention, just staring out the window, trying not to dwell on everything that had happened tonight.

Ash reached over and clasped my hand. "You can get a new car. Maybe one that doesn't glow in the dark."

I cut a sideways glance at him and just shook my head. "You don't understand. I always felt invisible in school. But that car was my way of shouting "Look at me!" and it worked." I smiled as I took a short stroll down memory lane. "Everyone thought it was so cool, and by extension, I was cool too."

"Maybe in high school. But you're a grown-up now. There must be a better way of standing out without driving a car that can be seen from blocks away. You might as well have drawn a target on yourself tonight."

As we got closer to home, our conversation abruptly ended. The streets were oddly clear of traffic, and there were fewer lights the closer we got. With only two blocks to go, all the streetlights went out. We could tell that some houses had lights on, but they fought to cut through the gloom that had settled over everything. The pall muffled even the typical night sounds.

"Something is not right," Ash said as if to not bring attention to us as the Tesla quietly reached our destination.

Nico's car slid in behind us as we pulled into the driveway. We sat, straining to hear anything. But the lack of sound was the least of the issues, if the two inugami creeping from the backyard were any indication.

CHAPTER 13

We sat stunned as the headlights illuminated the beasts. They were something out of a nightmare. Tall and broad, their red glowing eyes glared at us as we sat trapped in our cars. Ash was fighting his tiger for control. Shifting in the confines of the car would be a disaster. But they were too close and would have been on him in a heartbeat if he had tried to get out. Even if he started his shift as soon as he opened the door, the hounds would both be on him before he could finish it. Shifters are rugged, but they are not indestructible.

I could see in his eyes that he would try it, nonetheless. Grabbing his arm, I stopped him and pointed as our unlikely saviors rounded the building.

Magoo led the charge against the dogs as Uka followed behind, holding a sword in each hand. Standing straighter than I had ever seen, she raised one sword over her head and held the other across her chest. She was a sight to behold in her bathrobe and fuzzy slippers.

The dogs were distracted long enough for Ash to leap from the car and change. If I had thought his tiger striking when we were kids, it was nothing on the mature version. Dark black stripes formed a double loop pattern down his rich orange hide. Large amber eyes stared from a head so massive that I had no words for it. Turning in my direction, he raised a plate-sized paw and slammed the car door shut. This was his way of telling me to stay put.

I grabbed my purse from the car floor and took the revolver from the pocket designed to conceal it. Screw that. I was done being some whiny little bitch that needed to be saved.

Being a cop's daughter had its benefits. One of which was learning to shoot at a young age. Thinking I was a Null, my father wanted me to be able to defend myself. As soon as I was of legal age, I took the needed training and received my Concealed Carry License. Most days, I did not bother to arm myself, but tonight was different. I might have been rash and even foolhardy to go out by myself, but I wasn't stupid.

Opening the car door, I rolled out and came up in a crouch, aiming my gun at one of the beasts. I didn't need to roll out of the car. Okay, maybe I was stupid. But I felt so badass doing it this way. Until one of those things turned, swiping the gun from my hands.

Nico took that opportunity to jump over and block me as it swiped again. His shirt hung in shreds, and blood began to well from the wounds on his chest. I turned my head in time to see the second inugami toss my cat into the garage door, leaving a Magoo-sized dent.

The hound that Nico had been facing turned toward Uka, no longer seeing us as a threat. Arms were windmilling so fast I could hardly see them; I watched as she made the creature give ground to her strikes. But otherwise, her cuts seemed to make no impact on it.

Then I watched as the first inugami left Magoo's limp form and turned on Ash. They met midair and instantly became a whirlwind of teeth and hair. Frozen, I felt helpless as my friends defended me, and their blood stained the ground.

Rage began to build behind my eyes, and I raised my face to the sky, screaming. Heat crept up my body as I directed my gaze at the first one, then the other inugami ravaging those I cared for. Fire streamed from my out-thrust palm and collided with one of the creatures as it began to dive at Uka. Cold blue flames met it in flight, and I watched as it immediately turned to dust.

Turning my gaze at the one surviving hound, I watched in amazement as it crashed to the ground and seemed to melt before our very eyes.

Now that the threat appeared defeated, I felt more than saw everyone's gaze turn to me—even Magoo, who had picked himself up and was shaking the dirt from his coat.

Suddenly, I realized that I was looking down at everyone. Glancing around, it took me a moment to recognize that I was suspended about ten feet in the air. As soon as I did, I came crashing down onto the driveway.

I made a less-than-graceful landing (no surprise there) and ended up on my butt. Large amber eyes, set in the most handsome feline face, peered into my own. Seemingly satisfied with what he saw, Ash started sniffing me from the top of my head and all down my body. This must have been the Supernatural equivalent of a CAT scan.

Chuffing in my face, he moved over and let one ample paw rest on the car's trunk. Uka appeared to understand his need and reached into the driver's side door to release the trunk latch. Using his nose, Ash rummaged through it until he found what he needed. Grabbing a package wrapped in brown paper and string in his mouth, he stalked into the backyard. Moments later, a now fully human Ash came back around the corner, pulling a T-shirt over his head. Without a word, he grabbed his phone from the car and dialed.

"We need a containment crew here. Dumbrowski is down. Bring as much bagged blood as you can."

Dread settled over me, and I ran into the backyard before anyone could stop me. I had spent the last five years as an EMT and a paramedic. But none of that prepared me for what I saw next.

Those creatures had turned my ordinary, run-of-the-mill suburban backyard into a low-budget horror movie set. Body parts lay strewn across the spring grass, and blood was washed up the sides of my house. I found a leg with gnaw marks, and someone's head peered at me from under a bush. I closed my eyes to block the images from assaulting me. But the smell could not be stopped, and I felt my stomach rebelling.

Warm hands settled on my shoulders and turned me around. "Let's go in the house. One of my teams is on the way, and we'll only be in their way."

I let him lead me back toward my front door. "What are they going to do?"

"First thing will be to mask our surroundings so your neighbors don't see what is happening. It looks like whatever spell they used to cover the inugami's movements was starting to lift. It was probably broken with their deaths."

"Not dead. Inugami will be back," Uka said quietly, entering the house behind us. She held Magoo in her arms, and I cried with relief seeing them both.

Panic set in when I did not see my best friend. "Where's Nico? Someone find Nico!"

"Calm down, Tai. He's going to get some blood to help him heal. Those gashes on his chest were pretty deep," Ash informed me.

I sagged with relief. "What about the bodies in the back?"

Ash's lips thinned, and the first signs of anger appeared on his face. "Just one body. Sebastian Dumbrowski. One of my best people. I called him from the club to watch the house until we arrived. I don't know what made him engage the inugami. His job was to observe and report. Nothing more."

Uka laid one hand on Ash's arm. "Very brave. Took down one inugami alone. I was honored to fight beside him."

Wiping a hand down his face, he continued, "He's a vampire, so if we can find his head and torso, we might be able to revive him. That's why I had them bring so much blood."

"I think you'll find his head under my lilac bush." I gagged a little when I said that.

He unclipped a radio I hadn't noticed before and stepped away as he spoke to his team.

I needed to keep busy, so I made a pot of coffee and tea. However, my tea was just a few tea bags thrown into a water kettle on the stove. Uka might turn her nose up at it, but I no longer cared. Opening the fridge, I started pulling out cheese and all the makings for sandwiches.

Ash came back into the kitchen and made me sit down. "You don't need to feed everyone. They are here to do a job, not a party."

Just then, two men I had never met before came through the back door, and Ash directed them to my bathroom. I didn't get a good look at what they were carrying and didn't want to. Another team member came running in with a cooler of what I took to be bags of blood and headed after them. My bathroom was small, and

I thought someone would have to stand in the sink for everyone to fit in.

Ash handed me a hot drink. "Finish that, and then go pack an overnight case. You're coming home with me."

I looked over at where Uka stood, still cradling Magoo. Nodding her head at me, she said, "Do not worry about us, chan. We will take care of each other until you come home."

"What about Nico?" I whispered.

"I will take my dear ole mother up on her offer and join her at her hotel. I hear they have fabulous room service," my BFF answered from the doorway. He looked much better if you overlooked the shredded and bloodstained shirt.

I was torn. This was my home. But more and more, it was becoming a prison. However, I needed to figure out how to be in such proximity to Ash. The more time we spent together, the harder it was to ignore the old feelings rising inside me.

Ash turned me, so I was looking right at him. "It's just for tonight. I need to check on Sebastian, and we can go."

I put my empty cup aside and went to the bedroom to gather some things while Ash looked in on his team in the bathroom.

"Well, the good news is Sebastian is responding. The bad news is you better pack for at least two days. It will take that long to clean up the mess in there," he called to me.

I grabbed a couple more pairs of undergarments to go with the jeans and shirts I had already packed. When I returned to my bag, I found the load had been dumped out on the bed. Spinning around, I found Nico repacking everything neatly. I also discovered that he had left my jeans and added the white dress from the other night into the bag. Nico had also included some heels and a new pair of dress pants. Not to mention the silky nightgown he had given me as a birthday gift. I'd never worn it. I had no reason to.

"Now you're ready for a sleepover with that hunky piece of jungle cat in the other room," he proclaimed as he picked up the bag and headed out of the room.

CHAPTER 14

Grabbing my purse, I shoved a long T-shirt and leggings into it along with my jade bracelet. No way was I parading around Ash's condo in that little slip of fabric. Thank goodness for large purses. I could fit Magoo in here if I needed to. Not sure I could lift it, though.

The car ride to Ash's condo was completed in silence. He seemed deep in thought, and I did not want to disturb him. Plus, I was still trying to process everything that had happened this evening. Pulling into an underground garage, he grabbed my bag from the trunk as I hefted my purse onto my shoulder. I trailed behind him silently as we entered the lobby. A lobby with an honest-to-goodness doorman. Only this doorman was sitting at a desk, and from the amount of body hair I could see, he was very obviously a shifter.

Jumping to his feet, he tipped his hat to us. "Evening, Mr. Montgomery. Can I help you with the bag?"

"I'm good, Oscar. This is Ms. Jotun. She is going to be staying with me for a while. I want you to ensure that no one is told she is staying here."

Oscar threw a wink at us. "I understand completely, Mr. Montgomery."

Ash gave him a sour look. "I don't think you do. Ms. Jotun is under my protection as of this moment. No one who is unknown to you or any of the other guards comes or goes through this lobby without my authorization."

Huh…so they were guards, not doormen. That was interesting.

Straightening up, I fully expected him to throw a salute at Ash. "Yes, sir. I understand. Welcome to the building, Ms. Jotun."

Making our way to the bank of elevators, Ash took out a key and used it to open the door to one of them. I noticed only one button on the console when I entered the car.

He answered my questioning look. "I've got a penthouse." He shrugged and gave me a sly smile. "Money has its privileges."

I laughed for the first time that night. "Oooh…so I get to hang around with Mr. Hotshot?"

He laughed a little at that remark and led me down a brightly lit hallway once we reached the floor. We passed two doors before coming to his. The lights were already on when we stepped inside, and I gratefully dropped my purse on the kitchen table. I had not taken time to focus on the layout when I was here before. But now I glanced around the open floor plan, noticing how impersonal and cold the room felt.

"You don't spend much time here, do you?"

He led me down the hallway toward the bedrooms. "Only to sleep. I prefer spending time on pack grounds when I can."

His family had a sizeable wood-framed house in the pack compound. I remember it as being warm and inviting and full of laughter. It was the very opposite of this rather sterile environment.

Opening one of the bedroom doors, he ushered me into a room encompassing all the personality the rest of the place lacked. My feet immediately sank into the plush cream-colored carpet. Sheer drapes in pale pink framed floor-to-ceiling windows looking out over the city skyline. A brocade bedspread in shades of cranberry and tan graced a four-poster bed covered with myriad pillows in shades of pink and red.

Ash placed my bag on the bed. "This is Anika's room. Go ahead and borrow anything you need. She won't mind. The bathroom is through that door. The Jack-and-Jill bathroom connects to my parents' room. But you will have it all to yourself since they're not here."

He took my hand in his. "I'm right next door. Yell if you need anything."

I squeezed his hand before pulling mine away. "I should be fine. I'm just going to take a shower and go to bed."

He gave me a quick hug before leaving. "Sweet dreams."

91

I headed straight to the bathroom, stripping off my clothes. I neither cared nor even noticed the trail I left behind me. I focused on taking the world's longest and hottest shower, then climbing into bed. I groaned as I remembered Dr. Montgomery's instructions with the heart monitor. Short showers only until the monitor came off. So I made do with the world's hottest quick shower.

Wrapping myself in a thick bath towel, I realized that my purse and leggings were in the kitchen. Cursing the whole time, I gave in to the inevitable and donned the silk chemise-style nightgown Nico had given me. Turning to the full-length mirror on the back of the door, I critically looked at myself. I had to give it to Nico; he sure knew how to pick clothes for me. The nightgown was made of raw silk, between lilac and purple, in a muted color. Its simple lines fell straight to my feet and caressed my skin. I moved my hips side to side and relished the feel of it sensually brushing my curves.

The only blight to the picture was the monitor still taped above my breast. The edges on it were beginning to peel, and I played with them. I was tearing just a little here and there. The knock on the door made me jump, and I tucked my hands behind my back like a guilty child caught stealing candy.

"Tai, I just spoke to my parents. They said we could take the heart monitor off."

I didn't wait for him to say anymore. I grabbed the edge of the tape I had just been playing with and tore it off in one stroke. I hoped the walls in this place were soundproof because the scream I let out nearly shattered the windows.

I fell back on the bed, hands over the area where the tape had once been, as Ash flung the door open and raced into the room. Seeing me prone on the bed, he lifted me and helped me sit up.

"Tai! What's wrong?"

"I think at least three layers of skin came off with it," I murmured.

I felt him start to chuckle. "If you had waited a minute, I could have told you that my mom had a salve to help dissolve the adhesive."

I closed my eyes and leaned back against his chest, which I realized was naked. "Now he tells me."

He poked me in the ribs, where he knew I was ticklish. "And whose fault is that?"

I squealed as I did as a child when he would start tickling me. Slapping at his hand, I turned and tugged on his hair to stop him. This action encouraged him, and I found myself flat on my back as his fingers found spots that had me laughing too hard to fight back. One shoulder of my nightgown had slipped off, and my hem was hiked up around my thighs. My left leg wrapped around Ash's hip as I tried to get some leverage.

I don't know who stopped first, but I stared into his eyes. Long, impossibly long lashes framed his amber eyes, and I swear I could see his tiger staring out of them at me. His pupils dilated as he stared at my mouth.

"I don't think this is a good idea," I whispered, at the same time wishing he would keep going.

"I know," he said softly as his mouth claimed mine.

I wrapped my arms around Ash's strong neck and pulled him as close as possible. The heat from the kiss left a scorching trail from my mouth to my toes. I remembered that one brief kiss prom night. I had thought I was in heaven then, but it couldn't compare to this.

His fingers threaded themselves through my hair as our kiss deepened. Our tongues found each other and twined together in an erotic dance. I thought it couldn't get any better when he suddenly pulled away and nipped the sensitive area over my breast where I had torn the tape off. His hands began to slide under the gown's hem when his phone started vibrating from the pocket of his sweatpants. At first, I thought he was bringing something kinky into play. But then I heard a synthesized voice saying, "Your mother is calling." Talk about a mood killer.

"I wonder who that is?" I asked rather breathlessly.

"I better take this," Ash said as he reluctantly rolled off me and sat on the edge of the bed.

I propped myself up on one elbow and blatantly listened to his side of the conversation.

"No, Amma. I wasn't sleeping yet. Yes, I think Tai may still be awake." I tried not to laugh when I heard that.

He kept nodding and agreeing to whatever she was telling him. "I'll let her know. Yes...9:00 a.m. tomorrow. Love you too."

Tucking his phone back into his pocket, he dropped his head into his hands. "They will be here in the morning to review what they found and ask you some questions. You better get some sleep."

"But...," I began to protest.

"Go to bed, Tai. I'll wake you in the morning." He quietly got up and headed toward the door.

The minute he left, angry tears fell from my eyes. How dare he? To start something and then walk out of the room. It felt like a slap, like prom night all over again.

I pulled myself together and marched into the bathroom. Now that the monitor was no longer on my chest, I could take a cold shower.

The dream snuck up on me. There was no slow, quiet approach to the building this time. One minute I was closing my eyes; the next, I was standing inside a temple or shrine. I knew it must be the same building as all my other dreams because I could see out a door and recognize the scenery.

This time the red fox lay slumbering on the side of a giant golden statue of Buddha. The rest of the room was unadorned. All except for a small table that appeared to hold offering bowls. It was placed directly in front of the statue.

I felt like I was watching a play and waiting for the next act. I wasn't disappointed as the snow-white fox slunk into the room. This time I could count all nine tails that it wore. A figure in a simple kimono of red silk followed close behind. I could not see the person's face, as it seemed clouded. But the overall feeling I got was one of commanding power. I sank deeper into the shadows so as not to be noticed. But the deity, Kami, pierced me with a familiar yet strange look. She reached down as if to pet the white fox. But instead, she grasped it gently and raised it until standing before her was a woman in blinding white, from her hair down to her dress. Her nine tails still showed and swept a gentle arc through the air. Briefly touching foreheads, they turned to look at me. The woman slash fox sported delicate features that seemed carved of ivory where the

Kami's face was obscured. Crystalline tears hovered on the edge of her lashes.

"You do her a disservice. She is stronger than you know. But she is not strong enough in this form to handle what is coming. To save her, you must wake her."

I felt frozen into place as the woman in white glided toward me. She appeared to be searching for something in my gaze as she took my face between her hands. Nodding once, she kissed my cheek softly and whispered, "Forgive me," before turning to dust and floating away.

I woke to Ash holding my shoulders and shaking me. "Tai! Tai! Wake up. Please wake up."

I blinked at him a couple of times before pushing him away from me. "What? I'm awake!"

"I could hear you sobbing from the hallway. When you didn't answer my knock, I found you sitting here crying. I've spent the last few minutes trying to get you to wake up."

He tentatively reached out for my hand. "What was wrong?"

I pulled my hand gently out of his and shook my head. "It was a dream. I don't know how to describe it. But it felt so real."

"Maybe a shower will help. It's almost 8:00 a.m., and my parents will be here soon."

I threw back the covers, swung my legs off the side of the bed, and sat as I got my equilibrium back. I was no longer in the slinky nightgown. After my extended cold shower, I snuck back into the kitchen to retrieve my purse. So I was clad in a rather old oversized T-shirt that used to belong to my father.

Ash just stood with a curious look on his face. I had no idea why since this shirt covered me almost to my knees.

"What are you looking at?"

"Your tail," he said.

"What the hell are you talking about?" I asked as I jumped up and tried to see behind me.

Sure enough, a very bushy red-tipped tail protruded from the bottom of my shirt.

CHAPTER 15

I ran to the full-length mirror and pulled up my shirt. Turning first one way, then another, I could see the tail more clearly. About ten inches long, it was a mix of dark red and black except for the tip. That was bright red.

At first, I was thankful that I had forgotten to put panties on after my shower. Otherwise, the tail would have bunched up inside of them. But then I caught Ash's reflection in the mirror.

"Are you seriously staring at my ass?"

He flushed and turned away. "Sorry. But you must admit, it's pretty cute." Then he smacked himself on the forehead. "I mean the tail. You have a cute tail."

I just rolled my eyes. After last night, I was reluctant to accept his compliments.

"I think I better leave and let you get dressed," he muttered, turning toward the door.

"You'll get no argument from me," I muttered.

Turning back to my suitcase, I rummaged through it until I found a pair of leggings and a T-shirt. I needed somewhere for my new appendage, and I was reluctant to cut an actual hole in my favorite pants. It took me some time to find a pair of scissors small enough to open the seam on the back of the pants. I could fix a seam... I think.

I wasn't about to ask Ash to help me, so I put the leggings on and tried to hold on to the spot where the base of my tail hit it. Then I had fun trying to take them off and not lose track of that spot. I sat on the bed and opened the seam about four inches. Enough to get the tail through, but not so wide I flashed anyone else. Shimmying in them, I took a good look in the mirror. I might have been a tad high in the cut, but the overall effect was okay.

I might not have been able to wear any underwear, but I was damned if I was going to go braless. I quickly discarded the one I had on last night and thanked heaven that Nico had put another in my bag. Of course, this one pushed the girls up. Putting on the "Sarcasm—My Gift to You" T-shirt he had bought me, I had to pull and tug to keep from spilling out of the top.

Finally dressed, I sat on the edge of the bed. I was waiting for any indication that the Montgomerys had arrived. I had no desire to be alone with Ash. He might not have thought much about last night, but he nearly broke my heart again when he walked away.

Growing bored just sitting and waiting, I pulled out my new phone and texted Nico a shot of my tail.

It only took a moment before my phone rang. "Is that real?"

"Oh, yeah." I went on to fill him in on both the dream and my wardrobe dilemma. "What's next? Do I get my ears back too? Am I going to be cursed to wear a hat everywhere?"

"What ears!" he squeaked.

I don't think I ever filled him in on that little revelation my parents laid on me.

I started wailing, quietly, as I did not want Ash to overhear. "What am I going to do about tonight? I have to go in front of the council at 8:00. I look like some cosplayer."

"Let me think. Give me a minute."

I listened as he sucked on his teeth (a habit that was both endearing and annoying).

"You keep thinking. I have to go." A minute was about all Nico had since I could hear voices coming from the kitchen.

"Don't worry, sweetie. I'll come up with something."

After making kissy face noises at each other, I hung up the phone. It took a few minutes and a stern conversation with myself before I could open that door and walk into the kitchen.

I stopped dead in my tracks as six sets of eyes turned in my direction. Four belonged to various Montgomerys, and the other two to my parents. I looked questioningly at Ash, but he shrugged his shoulders.

"Mom, Daddy, what are you doing here?"

My mother rushed over and gave me a bone-crushing hug. And that's not a metaphor; troll hugs could actually crush bones.

"Robert and Sunitha called and told us about your meeting with the council. Something that you should have done last time we talked to you," my father scolded.

"I didn't want you to rush up here." I sighed.

My mother kept squeezing me. "Well, we're here now, and good thing. When they picked us up at the airport, Robert told us all about last night."

Ash drew their attention while I struggled to escape my mother's choke hold. "I'm afraid we can't let you stay at the house. It's too dangerous right now."

My father turned and faced him. "Now listen here. That is our home, and we're not going to let a bunch of steroid-infused devil dogs run us off."

"With all due respect—"

"Listen, young man, I may only be a quarter troll, but I can smash my way through a brick wall. I'll snap one of those things in half if they try anything again. We are not leaving our daughter here unprotected."

Desperate to divert the direction of this conversation, I spun in the middle of the room. "Doesn't anyone see anything different about me?"

Mrs. Montgomery gasped and rushed over for a closer look. "Oh look, Robert, her tail came back."

Now everyone was talking at once. When did it come back? How did it come back? I liked it better when everyone was focusing on my parents.

"Listen, it just showed up this morning. I went to bed tailless and woke up sporting this thing," I explained.

Mrs. Montgomery stepped in again. "Were you angry when you went to bed last night?"

"No." Yes, but they did not need to know that story. "Maybe it's a delayed effect from the fight."

"Avinash, please put on some coffee. Everyone, we brought sweet rolls with us. Let's all sit down and go over what we know so far." Mrs. Montgomery was always the calm and collected one. She also had a penchant for feeding people, which was okay with me.

Since the kitchen table was not large enough for everyone to crowd around, chairs were pulled into the adjoining living room and placed around the glass coffee table. I was regulated to one of those chairs since they were open in the back and I could put my tail through them.

Someone handed me a cup of coffee and a sweet roll while everyone gathered their food. Would it make me a terrible person if I hoped someone would spill coffee on Ash's white rug? Just a little.

They all found places to sit, and for a few minutes, all was quiet as we sipped our drinks and ate our rolls. Finally, Mr. Montgomery set his cup aside and looked at his wife.

"Do you want to start, or should I?" he asked.

She patted his arm. "You go ahead."

Speaking to the room, he started, "So Sunitha and I have always felt that Tai's natural abilities were suppressed. But we could never figure out why or how to unlock them. From what we've seen this past week, anger seems to be the key. But only when there is a clear and present danger."

Turning toward me, he asked, "When was the first time this happened? You mentioned you'd had above-human strength for a while. What brought that on?"

I felt all the blood leave my face. This topic was not something I wanted to relive. "I don't remember exactly. Sometime in high school."

"How could you not remember?" my mother asked. "It was prom night, and we caught some slimy wolf shifter pawing at her in the driveway."

My father puffed up his chest. "That's right. But by the time we got outside, she had already rearranged his face. From the looks of the car, probably thrown him into it too."

"I remember that night. Ash was so mad when he got home. He had just bought that car, and it had a dented hood and broken headlight," Mr. Montgomery added.

Huh… I didn't remember throwing Stefan around like that. Hurray for me.

"He told me that he'd been jumped by some thugs when he stopped to put gas in the car." I could sense Ash's anger building.

My dad laughed. "So he claims he fought off some gang when he was actually bested by a girl half his size."

Anika turned toward Ash. "See, I've been telling you that guy is a creep. But no one listens to me."

I'd had enough of this conversation and wanted nothing more than to disappear into the floor. But it wasn't over yet.

Ash came over and knelt in front of me. "What did he say to you?"

I tried turning my face away, but he wouldn't let me. "Please tell me."

I could feel the long-buried resentment well up inside of me. "That by giving Stefan the keys to your car, you also gave *me* to him. He called me null and void. That I should be happy that anyone would want someone like me."

As Ash talked to me, my parents turned identical piercing glares in his direction. "Is that why you never wanted anything to do with the Supe community? Why you've set yourself up working with humans?"

I raised my chin, relieved that the whole story was finally coming out. "Partly. But mostly because I never fit in."

Ash returned the judgmental looks that both sets of parents were giving him. "I would never do anything to hurt Tai. She's like another sister to me."

"And yet you tried setting up your own sister with him," Anika threw out.

"Avinash, explain yourself. What hold does this wolf have over you?" his mother questioned him.

"I owe him a life debt, Amma," he answered quietly.

His father started. "How? What happened?"

Ash sat back down. "One night, about fifteen years ago, Stefan and I were with some other shifters our age. We caught an unfamiliar scent and followed it." He shifted around in his seat, clearly uncomfortable. "I was full of myself and decided to charge ahead. Before the others could catch up with me, I had cornered a rogue bear shifter."

Pausing to collect his thoughts, he continued with the story. "He must have been over eight feet tall when he stood and clearly outweighed me. But I was young and felt invincible. I attacked him without waiting for backup."

His father started to speak, but Ash held up a hand to silence him. "Let me finish the story before I hear about how stupid I was."

"Before I knew what had happened, it had shredded my shoulder and thrown me into a tree." He stopped to take a sip of coffee. "Stefan and the others got there about that time. His wolf stood over me, protecting me since I couldn't even stand."

He rubbed his right shoulder as if remembering the pain. "The others drove it off, and Stefan carried me back to his parents' house. They were gone on pack business, and we made up some excuse as to why I needed to stay there for a few days so that I could heal. He basically saved my life."

His mother's lips were pressed so tightly together they practically disappeared. "We will discuss your reckless behavior another time."

"This debt has been repaid many times over, Ash. It is time to evaluate his value to your life now."

Ash nodded his head. "You're right, Father. I need to have a serious discussion with Stefan."

He stood and hugged his parents before turning to the rest of us. "Mr. and Mrs. Jotun, it's nice to see you again, but I need to go. The enhanced tapes from the night of the attack are ready, and I want to review the shots Tai got with her dashcam. So please excuse me. I will see you all at Verge tonight for the council meeting."

He left me stunned as he turned and walked out the door—no apology to me. No goodbye, breaking another piece of my heart.

CHAPTER 16

My parents refused to be scared away from the home they'd shared for over thirty years. I filled them in a little more on the past week's happenings on the drive home, marveling at how quickly one's life could be turned upside down. I borrowed a long skirt from Anika to hide my tail. Well, it was long on her 5'2" body. It didn't even come to my ankles. But it did the job, and I was less self-conscious.

I glanced at Uka's house as we pulled into the driveway but saw no signs of life. Worry started to claw at my throat, and I sprinted over there as soon as the car had stopped. I ignored my parents' calls and let myself into the house. The door was unlocked, and I let myself in to find…nothing. Absolutely nothing. The place looked deserted. The warm retro kitchen, I remembered, was still there, but dust and cobwebs covered it. The curtain separating it from the rest of the house was gone, and I could see straight into the living room. Racing through the house, I called out for Uka and Magoo both. But no one answered, and all I found were more cobwebs with no sign that anyone had lived there for many years.

My parents found me there, staring blindly at where I used to share tea with Uka. "Where could they be? Where is Magoo?"

"Magoo? You still had that mangy old cat? I would have thought it would have died by now," my father said, oblivious to my despair. I had some more explaining to do.

"Maybe they're at our house, honey. Why don't we go look?" my mother responded, guiding me toward the door.

We walked back and let ourselves in through the back door. I had to hand it to Ash and his crew. They had done a fantastic cleaning job. No trace remained in our backyard of the carnage, and the bathroom looked spotless. I checked to see if Uka had left a note, but nothing.

Daddy looked around the house. No amount of cleaning could remove the oppressive atmosphere that hung over it. "Your friend may be right. Why don't we check into a hotel for now?"

My mother shivered and wrapped her arms around herself. "I think that is an excellent idea. Tai, grab more of your things, and let's get out of here."

I decided to put my foot down. "No. You guys go ahead and take off. I'll meet you both tonight. But for now, I need some time to myself."

Pulling the curtains back, I pointed to the cloudless sky. "It's a bright sunny day, and I should be fine. I'll grab an Uber or a cab and meet you later. Text me when you're settled, and we can get dinner before the meeting."

My mother looked worried and glanced at my dad for support. "If you're sure…"

I walked over to the door and held it open while I made shooing motions. "Go. I promise it's okay."

I finally got them out the door and headed to my bedroom. Feeling restless, I began picking up and organizing my clothes. I imagined how each piece would look with a tail hanging out the back the whole time. I hoped that this was a temporary accessory.

I sank onto the bed and rested my head in my hands. I was royally screwed if we couldn't figure out where the tail had come from and how to get rid of it. There was no way I could hide it at work. That meant I'd have to quit the job I loved. Of course, the meeting tonight could make the whole thing moot if they decided I was a danger to the general population.

I tried calling Nico to tell him the house was as good as new. It was cleaner than it had been before the attack.

Finally, after a dozen rings, he picked up. "Can I call you back?" he asked breathlessly.

"No, this will be quick. The house is back to normal, so you can ditch your mom and come home."

I could hear a deep male voice in the background, and Nico giggled. "About that. I'm not exactly staying at the hotel."

"Then where are you?"

"Um…well, I stayed to help Ash's team last night. It was something to see how they were able to revive Sebastian. And I couldn't just leave the poor man alone. I mean, he risked his life for us. The least I could do was nurse him back to health."

I had to laugh. Leave it to my BFF to pick up a mortally wounded man…vampire, whatever.

"I thought you would help me find something to wear." I mean, funny as this was, I needed some help here.

"Since you're home, I'm sure you can throw something together." I could hear more talking in the background. "Gotta go. It's time for someone's sponge bath. Kiss kiss. I'll see you tonight."

I stared at the phone as he hung up on me. Tossing it aside, I dug through my closet. I pulled out and discarded about six outfits before I bowed to the inevitable and grabbed one of the new pairs of pants. Heading to my sewing box, I blew the dust off the top, rummaged for a needle and thread, and found my missing seam ripper when it stabbed me in the finger. Thusly armed, I went to battle with the pants. It took nearly an hour, but in the end, I had a pair of navy-blue dress pants that sported a reinforced opening in the back for my tail. Rummaging in my dresser drawers, I found a pair of thong underwear that were loose enough to allow me to push the thong portion around the tail without constricting it. Lastly, I pulled out a silk blouse in white that I could leave untucked without looking sloppy.

Exhausted and stiff from the night before, I headed into the bathroom. I stopped just short of the tub. I wanted to be able to soak in some hot water. But imagining what had gone on in my only bathtub twelve hours ago had me swearing off baths for the immediate future. Instead, I settled for a lengthy shower, though the water temperature cooled faster than I would have liked.

I spent a little more time on my hair and makeup than usual. Since I couldn't reproduce Nico's cat's-eye effect, I settled for giving myself a smoky eye, then layered on the mascara. Letting my hair dry naturally, I used the curling iron to give it a bit of volume. I dressed quickly, as I had lost track of time. Dusk was about to settle over the house when I completed my look with pearl stud earrings and a single pearl necklace. They had a slightly pink hue, and the gem nestled against the skin of my breasts.

Even though it was still unseasonably mild, I put on my lighter-weight winter coat since it was long enough to cover my tail. Feeling dressed for battle, I called my parents and told them to meet me at Verge before calling an Uber for myself. Locking the door behind me, I looked around my quiet neighborhood. It all appeared so normal. But my sense of security had been deeply affected last night, and I didn't know if I'd ever feel safe here again.

I endured the chatter from my driver as we made our way downtown. After leaving him a healthy tip and suffering one more story about his newest grandchild, I let myself into the foyer at Verge.

I no sooner put one foot in the door than my cousin Dunker accosted me. "Hey, Cousin Tai! How do you like my new glasses."

A pair of black-framed glasses was sitting right on his bulbous nose. They gave him a Buddy Holly look. However, no one could miss Sunreaver's as they looked like something Elton John discarded as too flashy.

"Wow, just wow. Look at you two." I didn't know what else to say.

Sunreaver beamed. "Yeah, Ma took us to get them. We can see real good now."

"Wow. They look...wow." I had to come up with a new word.

"Hey, Uncle Hank and Aunt Rachel are already inside. You want me to show you to their table?" Sunreaver asked. "Because I can see real good now and hardly trip over anyone anymore."

I didn't have the heart to tell him no. He was like a toddler—if that toddler were nearly seven feet tall and a troll.

"I would be happy to have such a distinguished escort," I said as he held his arm out for me to take.

"See. Tai thinks I'm distinguished." This made Dunker pout, and I had to throw a random compliment his way. Otherwise, I'm sure there would have been bad feelings between the brothers. And with trolls, that could lead to all kinds of property and bodily damage. I didn't think my insurance would cover it.

He led me around the dance floor's perimeter to a well-appointed table near the front. I was pleased to see my parents sitting with the Montgomerys. But that feeling disappeared when I saw that Viktor Asmuth was also at the table. Not wanting to appear rude, I took the remaining chair, which happened to be right next to him.

"Ms. Jotun. Such a pleasure to see you again. Your parents were entertaining me with stories of your childhood. May I ask, did you really try jumping out the attic window into a snow drift?" he asked as I settled myself into the chair.

I took a moment to glare at my mother, who was giggling like a teenager. "Yes, and I would have succeeded if old Mr. Bosworth from across the street hadn't seen me and called my parents."

He clapped his hands together and let out a hearty laugh. "Excellent! And they told me that the tail you had as a child had suddenly reappeared. I wonder why that is?"

Gratefully accepting the glass of wine my father passed me, I took a healthy swallow. "Yes, well, that is the question of the hour."

Viktor motioned to my tail. "Would you mind if I took a closer look at it?"

Mr. Montgomery nodded. "Yes, Tai. Let Viktor take a look."

My parents encouraged me, and I reluctantly stood so he could get a better look.

Holding it gently in his two hands, he commented, "How full and soft it is. Definitely a foxtail, but such an unusual coloration."

Taking an old-fashioned monocle out of his pocket, he examined it closer. It puzzled me how I could feel the cold radiating off his hands through the thick fur. It was all I could do to restrain myself from pulling it away.

"Yes, I'd hazard to guess that if you were to change into a true fox, you would be what is known as a black and orange. Quite rare."

His statement caught my attention. "So you think I may be a fox shifter?"

Putting the monocle back into his pocket, he gently released my tail. "No, my dear, I believe you are what is known as a kitsune."

Before he could explain more, a commotion from the back of the room caught our attention. Weaving through the dancers on the floor, a very intoxicated Stefan staggered toward us with Dunker and Sunreaver right behind him.

"You bitch! You think you're so special. Well, let me tell you. You're nothing! Nothing, do you hear me!" he yelled over the music.

Finally making it to our table, my cousins each took an arm to restrain him. "I'm sorry, Mr. Asmuth. He snuck past us while we were checking IDs."

Stefan tried shaking off their hands. But two trolls trumped one drunk wolf shifter. Thank goodness.

My parents stood and moved in front of me. It was a sight to behold to see my quarter-troll dad and half-troll mother lose all traces of their humanity when someone threatened their child.

"Sure, let someone else fight your battles. You're no better than a human. Too weak to fight for yourself."

I motioned my reluctant parents to step back and moved toward the now rabid wolf. "I don't need them or anyone to kick your ass, you mangy piece of shit. I did it once, and I can do it again."

I could feel that warmth rising within me, which I now understood was my burgeoning powers. But before I could unleash my anger at Stefan, I felt a hand on my shoulder, and a cool sensation sucked the heat at my core. I instantly began to relax. I hadn't noticed until then that the music had stopped, and dozens of faces were turned, watching the drama unfold.

"Tai, please allow me. I'd rather not see my place of business get in between you two," Viktor stated.

Raising one hand, he snapped his fingers, and an opaque dome settled over our immediate area. Once in place, I could faintly hear the music start playing again but couldn't see out of the shield to know if the other patrons had lost interest in us.

He held Stefan's gaze as he stepped around me and approached my antagonist. I could feel the power rising around us as he placed a finger on the shifter's forehead. "From this time forward, you are banished from this establishment. You may no longer cross its thresholds nor even speak its name."

He gave a slight push that nearly sent Stefan sprawling. "Leave."

The power behind that one word rocked the rest of us back onto our heels. Instantly, the dome sheltering us dropped, and our ears were assaulted by the pulsating music. Stefan appeared dazed, turned around without a word, and made his way to the front door. I could see him struggling once he reached it, but he couldn't overcome whatever compulsion Viktor had placed on him. I saw him give one final snarl before exiting the building.

We all resumed our seats, and I looked at Viktor Asmuth in a new light. "My apologies. I should never have responded to him the way I did. Verge is a place of business, not a back alley."

He gave me a large smile. "Apology accepted. I'm sure you would have handled yourself admirably. That youngling needs to be taught a lesson. But tonight is not the night to do it."

"I wonder what set him off?" Sunitha Montgomery asked.

"I believe that your son terminated his employment. Or, in the common vernacular, he canned him," Viktor provided.

I was shocked and pleased by this turn of events. But my pleasure was short-lived when Ash walked into the club with Melinda Paterson. I knew he had planned to be here for the hearing, but seeing them together made my stomach tense. It also reminded me of the seriousness of the gathering. I settled for sipping my wine while everyone else ate their meals.

The pair took a table not far from ours, and I watched as they put their heads together to talk. It looked all very cozy and intimate, making me want to vomit. Turning back to my table companions, I found Viktor watching me.

Seeing that our tablemates were otherwise engaged, he leaned in toward me. "Jealousy does not become you, my dear. I'm sure the young Mr. Montgomery's attention is solely focused on the upcoming gathering."

I looked closer at him, reminded that as young as he appeared, his archaic speech hinted at a much older man. Before I could voice a rebuttal, the pair in question stopped at our table.

Nodding greetings to everyone, Ash came to remind us of the time and waited as we gathered our personal belongings. Melinda led us toward the elevators as he put a hand on my arm to hold me back.

"Don't be nervous. I found some fascinating camera footage from the night you were attacked. We should also have the information from your dashcam shortly. My team was working on enhancing the image and will text it to me."

I gave him a small tight smile. "Thank you. You've been great. I know I am taking much of your time that is probably better spent elsewhere."

"And you won't need to worry about Stefan anymore. I gave him his walking papers and told him to stay away from you and Anika."

"Yes, well, he never did take instruction well. I've already had one run-in with him tonight."

Ash's eyes sparked with anger. But before he could say a word, Melinda stomped back to us. "Are you coming or not? The council does not like to be kept waiting." It was evident from the glare I received that she was unhappy with our *tête-à-tête*. Ash's guiding me to the elevator with his hand on my back earned me a full scowl from her.

As the door closed, I realized Viktor had never explained what a kitsune was or why he thought I was one.

CHAPTER 17

We exited the elevator into organized chaos. The pub-style and dining tables that had littered the floor were nowhere in sight, and in their place were about a dozen rows of chairs, five on each side of a central aisle. The buffet tables from the first night were pushed together and draped in crimson cloth. The French doors leading to the terrace were covered by heavy curtains that complemented the burgundy and cream-patterned carpet.

Once again, the room hosted a hodgepodge of Supernaturals. A family of gnomes—a mother, a father, and two children—were seated in the first row. Directly behind them sat a lone banshee, crying quietly into a handkerchief. I noticed a local coven member slipped into an aisle seat. She looked around and caught Ash's eye, giving him a brief nod before turning her attention to the front of the room. A man dressed all in black stood at the back of the room and did the same thing.

"What are all the looks about?" I asked him softly.

"Just a few of my people. Alpha Benton asked for some added security tonight," he explained, nodding at another man directly across from us.

Melinda left us standing there while she met with the uniformed guards standing behind the tables at the front of the room.

Our parents had arrived ahead of us and waved to get our attention. They had grabbed the very back row of seats and were holding court. I recognized more cousins as they chatted with my parents, and several younger members of the local pack vied for Anika's attention. The one person missing was Viktor Asmuth.

There was a great jostling at the front of the seating area as everyone seemed to jockey for position. But as it had been in school, I preferred the back of the room. Ash appeared to remember that as he deposited me a little way from our families and headed toward the front of the room. I took great pleasure in watching the others, trying to guess what had brought them here. I was confident that the gnome family was here to register their children with the council. If the children had been Null, there wouldn't have been any reason to be here. The council took very little interest in those that did not have any natural powers. The banshee may have been petitioning to move to another household, or perhaps she had a more private matter to discuss. But probably not. Otherwise, she wouldn't be here in front of such a crowd.

I felt a nudge at my side as I watched a rather tall man try to make himself comfortable in a middle row. "Wow. I didn't know the Bucks had a giant for a forward," Nico whispered as he sat down next to me.

"Only makes sense," I retorted. "Where have you been? I was starting to think you were going to abandon me."

"What can I say? At least one of us is getting lucky."

"How do these things normally work?" I inquired, trying to divert his attention away from my miserable love life.

We were momentarily interrupted as the council representatives entered the room in no particular order. Since we were in his territory, Alpha Benton took the center seat. On his right was Nico's mother. At the end of the table, slightly apart from the others, sat the mysterious elven member I had met at Bagha. I looked closely at the rest of the council members as they filed in. I could only identify a few; an orc took the other seat next to the Alpha. The mermaid was easy enough to determine by her greenish complexion and the iridescent scales covering her head instead of hair. I was sure the crone beside her was Baba Yaga, a Slavic witch. The rest were too human looking for me to recognize, at least from this distance.

Nico's attention wandered, as it was wont to do. He tugged at my sleeve and pointed to a couple about three rows in front of us. The woman was beyond nervous, fidgeting with her hair and her clothing. When the man beside her turned, I could tell he was a young vampire. From how he tried to calm his companion, I thought she was human. Such unions were not unknown but unique enough to warrant interest. My curiosity peaked, but a commotion at the front of the room drew my attention before I could speculate.

"Everyone, please quiet down and take a seat. We will begin the proceedings shortly." Alpha Benton banged a gavel on the table, effectively ending the networking portion of the evening. It was like watching an extreme version of musical chairs. A few of Anika's admirers ended up sitting on the floor. Each took sneaky glances at her when they thought no one was looking.

I focused my attention on the front of the room and noticed that one of the council chairs was empty. Having stepped away from this world for so many years, I was no longer aware of who the current council members were. But from what little I had learned recently, it appeared that the leprechaun councilman was the one that was missing.

We saw the Alpha motion to Melinda. They spoke quietly for a moment before she turned and left the room. It was hard to tell, but he looked worried. Facing the now-seated crowd, he cleared his throat.

"Please remain seated until your name is called. When you're done, you are free to leave." He glanced down at something in front of him. "Would Gidget and Elfi Boonswine please approach us?"

The gnome couple hurried forward, dragging their reluctant children behind. Mama Boonswine spat in her hand and slicked back the hair of one of the children while Papa straightened the other's jacket.

"Mr. and Mrs. Boonswine, it says you are here to register your children?"

"Yes, Your Honor…sir. This is Herble and Helna," the father stuttered. "They are ten years old and show all the traits of full gnomes."

Supes matured at different rates. But once they go through puberty, they must register with the appointed governor of the area. In this case, Alpha Benton.

He smiled down at the children. "Please come closer, kids, and introduce yourselves."

The little boy, who would have barely come to my knees, was the first to stand forward. "My name is Herble Boonswine, and this is my sister, Helna." His sister performed an obviously rehearsed curtsey, as you could see her mother coaching her through it.

"Well, Herble and Helna, do you agree with your father that you are full gnomes and ready to assume all responsibilities associated with that?"

The children looked confused until their father gave them a smile and nod. "Yes, Alpha Benton. We promise to be decent gnomes, listen to our parents, and be good to the land," they recited together.

The Alpha smiled down at them, then motioned the parents closer. "Your registration has been approved. Please follow this young lady, and she will complete the process. Then you will be free to go."

A girl who appeared to be about eighteen led them off to the side, where another table had been set up. The children would have an aural scan done to keep on file. I presumed that the older woman seated at the table was a member of the local coven. They were in charge of performing and safeguarding the scans. These scans were as accurate in identifying an individual as a fingerprint. But if they were to fall into the wrong hands, a person's identity could be stolen more thoroughly than any credit card theft.

They needed to pass the end of the table where the elven delegate sat, away from the others. As the gnome family passed by, the little girl turned to her mother and, in a voice that I believe she thought was a whisper, said, "Why does that man stink?" I loved that children had no filters as long as their comments were not directed at me.

Everyone turned in that direction to see him lift his lip and snarl at her. Father Gnome looked ready to throw down, but their escort hurried him along, and the incident was forgotten. Or maybe not, as time after time, the delegate was given a wide berth by the people ushered past him.

It was fascinating to watch. I was right about the banshee. She asked permission to leave her house and immigrate back to her native Ireland. As luck would have it, one of the council members present was the kelpie I had seen that first night, though she appeared to be dry this time (i.e., not dripping water all over the table).

Anika's fanboys were there for a complaint brought by a landowner that lived near pack lands. A Native American of the Ojibwe tribe, he was well aware of the Supernatural community and generally lived in harmony with it. But according to his account, he had suffered the loss of livestock by several wolves' continued harassment of his herds. He identified them by specific markings on their coats and had petitioned the council for reimbursement of his damages. Judgment was made in his favor, and the council also put the young shifters under a geis that would keep them from being able to shift for three months. Each shifter accepted their sentence with surprising grace, going so far as to apologize to the landowner individually—all under the watchful eye of their Alpha.

At last, the room had nearly emptied when Alpha Benton called my name. "Tai Jotun, please step forward."

I tried to walk calmly to the front of the room, but I could feel my legs begin to shake. Standing in front of the man who had helped raise me for three years, I calmed as I looked into his kind brown eyes. It also helped me know that I had friends and family behind me, cheering for me. That all flew out the window as soon as I heard Vanessa Rodrick speak.

"Taisetsuna Jotun, you are called before the council this day with the charge of manslaughter and failing to inform your governor of your change in status. In this case, you can no longer qualify as a Null. What have you to say?"

I stood silent in front of the table, overcome with a stench that made my eyes water. I had no idea how any of the council could have sat through all the proceedings with it wafting around them. It smelled like someone that had decided to marinate themselves in the most intense cologne they could find. But underlying it was another scent that played at my memory. I tried my best to ignore it while I defended myself.

"I was only protecting my life against an unprovoked attack." That was all I could get out before she grabbed the gravel from the Alpha's hands and banged it repeatedly on the table.

"Irrelevant! Your actions caused the death of a human and subjected us to scrutiny by the human police. Thankfully, we have enough connections in the department that the death was classified as a heart attack. Your reckless actions caused that man's death. I do not believe for a moment that he was anything other than human. You took your anger out on the first person you saw that night."

Again, I had no time to form a coherent answer before she banged that gavel. I was ready to grab the thing and pound her with it. But that wouldn't have helped my case. The other council members, except the elven delegate, seemed less than thrilled. He sat with his eyes focused on me and a smirk on his face.

Her voice suddenly took on a syrupy sweetness that worried me more than her yelling had. "Is it not true that you have been the victim of several more attacks since that night?"

I waited a moment to ensure she would give me a chance to answer. "Yes, ma'am. In fact—"

Again, she interrupted me. "Funny, there have never been any reports of these 'in-u-gamis' before that night. How do we know you aren't controlling them? Perhaps this whole thing has been staged." Protests erupted in the back of the room. It took a couple of Bagha security people, along with Nico and the Montgomerys, to keep my parents from storming to the front. Alpha Benton wrestled the gavel back from Nico's mother. "Quiet! Settle down before I have everyone removed."

"Alpha, Council Members, I have some evidence that could help in this case," Ash said as he (finally) stepped forward.

As a projector screen descended from the ceiling, he motioned for someone to turn down the lights. "I'd like to show you some footage that our cameras were able to catch on the night that Tai was attacked."

After tapping on the computer, a grainy image appeared on the screen. "As you remember, Verge's security camera's malfunctioned around 9:00 p.m. that night. Thankfully, I had some of my Bagha's camera's covering the building's exits."

"This first image shows the person who attacked Ms. Jotun directly in front but across the street from the club," he continued.

A new image appeared when he tapped a key. "If you look closely, you can see a black shape hovering directly over him."

He slowly advanced the rest of the images, taking time so that everyone could get a clear look at them. I was surprised when the final shot showed me as I was pulled back into the alley.

"As you can see, this black shape seems to merge with him. His posture and demeanor change, and he heads directly to the alley. You can also see the last image supports Tai's claim as he is clearly overpowering her."

"You said you had cameras on all of the exits?" the orc delegate asked.

"Yes, and each one shows something similar. In one, we see a human walking into the shadows near the south door. The third camera caught something akin to what I just showed you. Someone walking nearby and a dark shadow hovering over the human until he suddenly changed direction and situated himself near the east door."

This time Baba Yaga chimed in. "What significance does this hold?" Her voice was old and scratchy, reminiscent of pieces of parchment paper rubbing together.

Ash motioned for the lights to be raised and shut his computer. "Both of these people have in common that they left the area simultaneously. The time stamp on all the videos coincides with Tai taking down her attacker. We believe that these inugami possessed multiple people that night in hopes of attacking someone. Probably one of the council members. But Tai was the first one to exit the building."

Vanessa Rodrick sneered. "We only have your word on that." She turned to address the others. "I find it highly suspicious that we only see select photos instead of the whole video. How do we know it hasn't been doctored?"

Ash's color rose into his face, and his eyes started to glow at the challenge she had thrown at him. "All unaltered videos have been forwarded to your emails so that you might take a closer look. I will leave you to draw your own conclusions."

"Is this all the evidence you have, Ash?" the Alpha asked.

We all heard Ash's phone begin to ring, and he extended his apologies before stepping to the side to take the call. I stood awkwardly, trying to decide what to say or do with my hands. Ash returned to my side with a grim look on his face.

"That was the team I had working on the video that Tai captured the night she was followed and her car was rammed."

He turned toward the far end of the table. "Councilman Daecer, would you care to tell us why I have your personal car on camera that night, stalking Tai?"

The elf spoke for the first time that evening. "Lie," he growled.

His breath was enough to knock me down, and I stood at least twenty feet away. I felt sorry for the other council members sitting at the table. But the smell triggered the memory of my talk with Uka.

I grabbed Ash's sleeve. "Wet dog and decay. Uka said they smell like wet dogs and decay."

We turned as one to look at Daecer as he bolted for the back stairs.

CHAPTER 18

I even surprised myself when I was the first to run and reach him before he got through the exit door. But he turned and shoved me right into Ash, knocking us both back enough to give him time to start down the stairs.

Two of Bagha's security people raced past us as we heard yelling and loud animal-like growls echoing from the stairwell. Hurrying behind them, we were in time to see my cousins hold the fae by his collar at the bottom of the stairs.

Viktor paced around him, stopping to lean in and sniff despite the fae's continued struggles. Finally, I saw him place a finger in the center of his forehead, just like he had with Stefan. "Sleep, inugami," he commanded.

Ash and I made it to the ground floor to find Ailman Daecer out cold on the floor. The pounding of feet brought our attention back to the top of the stairs, where the other council members followed. Nico and my parents crowded the doorway behind them.

Viktor motioned to Dunker to pick up the unconscious delegate. Without effort, my cousin hoisted him over his shoulder and looked to his employer for instructions.

"What would you like done with him, Alpha? I can put a leash and collar on him if you want."

Viktor found this hilarious. But we were going to have to explain it to the rest.

"Bring him back upstairs please. Mr. Montgomery, do any of your supplies include iron?"

Ash got on his radio and instructed one of his people to bring up some iron chains.

The Alpha nodded his approval. "Prepared as always. Good. Now if everyone would please return to their seats, we will see if we can sort this out."

Filing up the stairs behind Ash, I admired how his jeans fit. I never could understand the trend where grown men wore oversized pants that slid down their butts. Of course, not every man could pull off tight pants. Ash could. Too bad he was such an ass.

"Perhaps if I traded my dress pants for jeans, I could get women to look at me like that," Viktor whispered.

I could feel myself turning red, and I hurried up the stairs as I heard laughter behind me.

Once we were back upstairs, Dunker dumped the elven delegate into a front-row chair while security brought chains to bind him.

"Ash, please have your people wrap some cloth around the chains. I don't want to injure our colleague, just hinder him," Alpha Benton instructed.

He turned to Viktor. "Mr. Asmuth, did I hear you say *inugami*?"

Viktor continued to pace around the newly bound fae. "Yes, Alpha. I am familiar with the creatures."

Turning to me, he asked, "And how could you tell that this *thing* was not Councilman Daecer?"

Viktor was now crouching in front of the chair. "Oh, but it is Councilman Daecer. The inugami is possessing him, and from the smell, he has been controlling him for a while."

At Alpha Benton's quizzical look, I jumped in, "They have a distinct smell. Like wet dog and decay."

He nodded. "That would explain his sudden liking for colognes. He was trying to cover it up."

Melinda chose this moment to burst through the door to the other stairway. She was agitated as she passed right by the bound delegate without a single glance. Hurrying to the reseated council members, she addressed the ensemble at large.

"I have not been able to locate Councilman O'Sullivan. My team and I have been through his hotel room and questioned the staff. The last time anyone saw him was around 10:00 p.m. last night."

The kelpie delegate jumped to her feet. "Have you tried tracking him?" She was obviously worried about her fellow countryman.

"We have some bloodhound shifters working on that now. But they haven't been able to pick anything up yet."

I sensed the growing unease as the delegates shared anxious glances.

"Alpha, perhaps it would be best if the rest of you stayed together until we know what is happening," Ash suggested.

The Alpha nodded his head. "Yes. We have sufficient room in the pack houses to accommodate everyone. Ms. Paterson, please assign each member security detail while they gather their things and have my Beta assign them housing within the pack grounds."

He turned to me. "Since this seems to corroborate everything we have heard tonight, you are free to go."

Vanessa Rodrick jumped to her feet. "I must protest. Whether or not an inugami was involved, she is still responsible for the death of a human."

Once again, I was kept from saying anything. Only this time, it was not the sound of a banging gavel that drew our attention. But the doors to the terrace were blown open by a strong wind that surrounded us with the smell of cherry blossoms. I nearly fainted with relief when I saw Uka and Magoo walk into the room.

I wanted to race and embrace them. But instead, I watched as, step-by-step, Uka began to transform. At first, it was as simple as her posture changing, no longer displaying the hunched form of an older woman. Her hair began to darken and grow. Within two steps, it reached her now slim waist. The ubiquitous cotton pants and tennis shoes she always wore transformed into a kimono of dark red silk, and traditional geta sandals graced her feet. At this point, Magoo raced ahead of her and jumped straight into my arms, nearly knocking me over.

Everyone stared mesmerized at the woman making her way to my side, but I noticed Viktor quietly exited the room. This was the same woman who appeared in my dream. Of that, I was sure. She turned me to face her as she reached my side. Despite the transformation, the eyes looking into mine were Uka's. She cupped my face with both of her hands and placed a kiss on my forehead.

Sunitha Montgomery was the first to approach us. "Inari Ōkami, welcome," she said in a respectful tone as she bowed from the waist.

Her words broke the spell holding everyone else in thrall. I heard the rustling around us but stood transfixed. I knew that the Japanese term *kami* meant "deity." So who or what was she?

"So the transformation has finally begun," she commented, in a voice no longer colored by the dryness of great age. It also lacked the heavy accent that Uka's speech always carried, an accent for which I constantly teased her.

She took Magoo from my arms and placed him on the floor. He immediately took up a protective stance at my feet. Both tails wrapped around my ankles as if he needed to maintain physical contact between us, and I had no complaints.

Her tone became harsh and angry as she turned to the council members. "Why are you persecuting this child?"

Alpha Benton stood to address her. "Mistress Inari, while we are honored by your presence here, I must protest. This transformation you just referred to is concerning. We are attempting to ascertain Tai's ability to continue to live and work in the human sector. We need to make sure she is in full control."

Councilwoman Ricard had to make her opinion heard. "There was also a human who died due to her actions."

Inari (I still can't wrap my head around that name) blew a soft breath into her hand and produced a fireball similar to the one I'd done that night. Only hers glowed in shades of crimson and gold. She never took her eyes off the Alpha as she tossed it toward Nico's mother, striking her in the chest. The effect was immediate, and Vanessa Rodrik danced like a marionette on a string, finally collapsing back into her chair. Shaking herself, she glared at those people trying to hold their mirth.

"As you can see, fox fire has only a mild effect, even on humans. That is not what killed the person. It was the fox fire forcing the inugami from them. Place the blame on the person who controls them, not on someone who was only defending themselves."

As if on cue, Ailman Daecer woke from his stupor. "In Oberon's name, release me this instant!" he snarled.

Like Viktor, she walked to the bound fae and touched his forehead. Using no words, she put him back into a deep sleep. Protest rose from the rest of the council. "Do not believe the creature. He uses your friend's voice to lie."

Ash stepped forward. "Ma'am, the other two humans I have on video did not seem to suffer any ill effect from their possession. Why did this man die?"

"Humans are weak creatures, and this one may have already been weaker than most. The shock may have been too much for them. Even if the fire had not forced it out, there is no telling if he would have survived the possession," she told us all.

It did go a fair way to assuaging my guilt. But I still had so many questions. "Why was I able to produce that fox fire? I'd never shown any indication of having any abilities at all."

She bestowed a smile filled with pride on me. "You are finally coming into your powers. They had been suppressed for so many years, and I had no way of knowing if you would ever be able to enjoy them."

"Enjoy? Uka... Inari, how can I enjoy something I cannot control?" I was genuinely perplexed and more than a little agitated. "Maybe if someone had warned me this might happen, I could have managed it better. But obviously, there are many things you need to explain!"

Mrs. Montgomery gasped and hurried to my side. "Tai, show some respect."

A pained look settled onto Inari's face. "Please do not scold her. She is right that I owe her an explanation."

"And I want to know why you have been stalking our daughter all these years," my mother exclaimed as she came up behind me and pulled me within the shelter of her arms.

"Please, Rachel. Be at peace. I would die before I would let any harm come to her."

"But why?" my mother insisted.

"Because she is my granddaughter."

CHAPTER 19

Granddaughter, the word rang in my ears. Have you ever felt as if your whole body, even your lips, had gone numb? At this point, I could only stare at the person I had considered my friend. I pulled away from my mother's embrace, suddenly finding it stifling. Looking around, I took note of the stunned expressions on the faces around me. But nowhere did I find a port in this storm that swept me along.

At last, I found refuge in Nico as he turned me around and looked into my eyes. "Hello…is anybody in there?" He gently slapped my cheeks.

Taking a deep breath, I fought to center myself. "Try that again, and you'll find out," I said, giving Nico a shaky smile.

"That's my girl," he whispered as he gave me a big hug.

Vanessa began spouting off some nonsense. Perhaps about me, maybe about global warming. I no longer cared.

"Can it, Mother," Nico snapped at her. The look on her face was priceless.

This time it was Alpha Benton wielding the gavel that brought me back to my senses.

"I suggest we proceed as planned. Ms. Paterson, please see to the arrangements I mentioned. Tai, you and your parents are welcome to also shelter with us on the pack lands until we know more about what is happening. Mistress Inari, may I extend the same invitation to you? A change of scenery will facilitate a more productive dialogue."

She acknowledged his invitation with a sharp nod but kept her eyes trained on my face. "Perhaps you're right. We can discuss this matter later."

Later was fine with me. Never would have been even better.

The orc scowled at the room in general. "What should we do with Daecer? Can we get rid of the inugami without hurting him?"

Inari answered him cautiously, "Yes, but it will take time to separate the two without damaging the fae."

"If I may make a suggestion?" Ash asked as he stepped forward. "In all the times we have encountered these creatures, there have never been more than three. It would be a safe assumption that that is all the magic user can handle. If we were to draw the other two out and capture them, the loss would severely cripple this person. We stand a good chance at learning the why behind these attacks."

He looked at Inari. "Is there a way to capture these things and confine them?"

She looked at him thoughtfully. "Yes...we might be able to bind them in a shokan sukura." She looked at the seated delegates. "A magic circle. Baba Yaga, would you be able to create a circle strong enough to hold them?"

"Of course, I can. Nothing I bind can escape until I release the circle." The old witch let out a cackle that was both spine-tingling and cartoonish.

"There is your answer, neko," Inari said.

Ash got a thoughtful look on his face as he rubbed his chin. "So we need to bait the trap and draw them in. But what do we use?"

Every eye turned to me simultaneously. "Well, shit."

One thing I was grateful for that evening, Inari was able to make my tail disappear. Or, more accurately, she taught me to concentrate, make it disappear myself, and repeatedly reappear until I wanted to cut the damn thing off. Of course, now I stood with a big gaping hole in the back end of my pants and nothing to fill it.

If only I could make the ears go away. Yep, during the makeshift education, I manifested fox ears. No matter how hard I tried, I could not get them to vanish, and she refused to do it for me. Nico promised to bring me some club wigs so I could go out in public.

By the time the plan had been hammered out, it was closing in on 2:00 a.m., and I was beyond exhausted. I graciously accepted the Alpha's offer of shelter for the night. But since the plan entailed resuming a (semi) regular routine, I'd have to return to my house. With Nico amid a fresh love affair, he would be staying with his new paramour, and it was decided that Ash would take his room in my house. Oh yippee… We made a veritable caravan as we traveled north to the pack's territory. I rode with my parents, who dropped me off at the Alpha's house. They were staying with the Montgomerys, and I had wanted some distance from Ash. Inari had granted me a reprieve when she declined Alpha Benton's invitation. I was relieved but knew it wouldn't last. A meeting was scheduled for noon the next day or today since it was nearly morning.

Pulling up to the imposing log home where I'd be staying for now, we were greeted by Alpha Benton's wife, who was also the pack's Luna. Wrapping me in a familiar baby powder–scented hug, I was immediately put at ease and led to the room where I used to stay. She had laid out an old-fashioned cotton nightgown and slippers for me. She provided a makeshift litter box for Magoo.

Magoo had not left my side and refused to be separated from me. Of course, I probably would have fought myself if anyone had tried. Surprisingly, no one mentioned one word about his second tail, and he was welcomed into the Alpha's home as if he were part of the family.

Sleep eluded me, despite my exhaustion. I managed a light doze on and off but finally gave up as soon as the sun began to rise. I was able to slip out of the house without waking anyone. Even Magoo was sleeping too hard to notice. Still, after so many years, I remembered my way to the bluff that overlooked Lake Michigan. I sat on the damp ground against a fallen log near the edge and watched as the rising sun painted the skyline and banished the night's shadows. The cresting waves sparkled with the new day's light, and I felt myself at peace for the first time since everything had started to change.

I listened as birds greeted the sun with their songs and heard small creatures scurrying through the decaying vegetation under the budding trees. Waves crashing on the rocks created a calming rhythm that began to lull me until I was startled awake. I'm unsure what roused me, but I no longer heard birds or rustling noises. The land had gone quiet, the sound of the water the only thing breaking the silence. I felt my new ears twitch and swivel like a cat when they caught the faintest hint of a footfall. That was my only warning before I was picked up and thrown like a rag doll.

I managed to land on all four feet (four feet?), and I had only a moment to digest that information before I saw a massive shifter charge me. Instinct took over, and I jumped into the air, amazing myself when I sailed right over it.

"Bitch. Think you're too good for me. Get me fired from my job. I had Ash in my back pocket. I could write my own ticket. Now I'm out. All because of some trashy piece of ass." The wolf's muzzle strangely distorted the words. It was Stefan, and he was in midshift and reeked of alcohol.

I was trapped. Stefan stood between me and the path back to the house. Behind and to each side, I was presented with a sheer drop down to the water's edge, where sharp rocks lay. In this form, I couldn't speak, so I stood mutely, waiting for his next move.

He paced back and forth in front of me, waving an empty whiskey bottle. "Look at you. Mooning after Ash all these years. I need to teach you how a real man does things."

Finishing his shift, I saw madness in the depths of his red eyes. The slightest tensing of his shoulders warned me he was about to spring again, and I prayed I could recreate that initial jump. If I could figure out how I had managed to fly that night we were attacked, I could keep myself out of reach.

I crouched and sprang up as he began his charge. Thankfully I could jump high enough that he wouldn't be able to reach me. Unfortunately, I couldn't maintain it and crashed onto his back. I let instinct take over again and bit down as hard as I could on the back of his neck. Hot blood gushed into my mouth; it was all I could do to keep from gagging.

He reared up on his hind legs and tried shaking me off, all the while howling in pain. When that did not work, he began to roll on the ground, finally scrapping me off on the fallen log. I wobbled to my feet again and found myself no better off than when I had started. Pain coursed through a back leg that had gotten twisted underneath me. But I was able to roll to the side as he charged again and raked his side with the rather impressive claws I now sported.

A plan began to formulate in my brain as desperation breathed down my neck. I started whining, acting as if my leg hurt worse than it did. As Stefan feinted and snapped at me, I let him drive me toward the bluff's edge. I conjured small orbs of fox fire, pelted him with them to keep him angry, and dragged the back leg in a show of weakness.

We inched closer until I finally felt the dirt shift under my back feet. Time seemed to stand still as we stared into each other's eyes. Triumph warred with the madness I'd seen in him, and I watched as his muscles tensed, preparing to lunge.

I caught movement at the edge of the tree line. I spotted Inari watching, with Ash and Magoo at her side. There was no time to ponder the implications as Stefan began to move. Praying that I had not overestimated my reserve strength, I let him get within inches of me before I sprang straight up into the air. Agonizing pain lanced through the injured leg, but I managed to stay aloft long enough for him to pass under me and over the bluff. I heard his scream as I came crashing back down to earth.

Magoo sat atop Ash's tiger as I blearily saw them fight against an invisible barrier. "Thanks for the help," I managed to croak as I lay facedown in the grass.

Glancing over my shoulder, I watched as Inari calmly made her way to me while the other two were freed from the restraint and raced over. Behind them came a cadre of pack members. Then I noticed I was again in my human skin, and the damn tail was back. I was also as naked as the day I was born. I lay as still as possible while Ash took his cold nose and tried to turn me over.

I refused to move and weakly swatted at him. "Leave me alone. Unless one of you carries an extra set of clothes, I'll never move from this spot again."

I saw Magoo peering over the bluff's edge, where Stefan had disappeared. "Splat." He giggled as various pack members began descending the cliff.

I felt the cool caress of silk on my back where Inari had draped a kimono over me. She stood between Ash and me to preserve my modesty as I sat up, slipped the robe over my shoulders, and tied it. "I'd say thank you, but I'd rather say, *What the hell?*"

"You stood back and watched. That maniac could have killed me!" I shouted. I stood and gingerly tried to put weight onto the injured leg.

Inari's expression changed to one of pride. "This was not our battle to win. You did well, granddaughter."

I stifled a cry when Magoo started to wind between my ankles. Stumbling into Ash, I saved myself from falling. But I still needed to learn how I would return to the Alpha's house. Sensing my pain, Ash presented his back and lowered himself enough that I could lay along his back. Circling my arms around his massive neck, he slowly stood. I let my head rest between his shoulder blades and closed my eyes while we slowly made our way back.

We were met by the whole pack when we reached the house. My father was the first to rush forward and gently lifted me from Ash's back. He carried me through the entranceway, then another door at the back of the foyer, into a doctor's examination room. My mother pushed him aside after he sat me on the exam table. She ran her hands over me, assuring herself I was in one piece.

"I'm fine, Mom. Just a pulled muscle, I'm sure." I couldn't mask the pained expression that crossed my face when she reached my left leg.

"You'll let me be the judge of that," Mrs. Montgomery announced as she shooed my parents out of the room.

She did a more professional examination than my mother had. But it still caused me pain when she reached the injured leg. "I'm going to give you a muscle relaxer and see if that helps. If not, we will need to take you to the infirmary, where I can get a CT scan and ensure you did not tear anything."

The shot took effect almost immediately, and I finally fell into a deep sleep.

CHAPTER 20

I discovered no escape in my dreams. Finding myself at the edge of a beautifully landscaped koi pond, Inari sat beside me in her Uka skin.

"Why are we here, and what's with the old lady's disguise?" I sighed.

"You seem to respond better to this image of me, chan," she said, though without the horrible accent she used to have.

"That's because Uka was my friend. I don't know who you are. You say you're my grandmother, but I find that hard to believe."

She bowed her head. "I am very sorry to have deceived you. But it was necessary. I did not know if you would ever come into your powers, and I wanted to ensure you were safe."

I turned to look her in the face. "Who am I?"

"That is what I have come here to show you." She slowly waved her hand over the surface of the pond. "Watch as I explain."

Images began to rise from the depths of the water. I saw a younger version of Inari sitting in a meadow, a young fox frolicking around her. Suddenly the fox turned into a little girl with raven hair. "Many years ago, too many to count, I created a child from the fox you see here. She was the first kitsune and was as close to a daughter as I would ever have. As she grew, we enjoyed many years of companionship, but she yearned for more of her kind."

She waved her hand again, and another scene presented itself. Now there were many foxes in the meadow, and the first one sported two tails. "I created more kitsune, and they became my children. But the first, Nasuki, was my favorite. She was your mother. I gifted her a small trinket, a heart made of jade with the word Taisetsuna carved into it. The same one you are now wearing."

130

Clutching at the jade charm, I peered closely at the undulating image in the water. It was hard to tell, but I wanted to believe that I could see some of myself in her, even in her fox form.

"There are times when this world becomes too much for me, and I must return to mother earth to rest. During those times, my kitsune became my eyes and ears. The freedom this presented overwhelmed some, and they never strayed away from our homeland. Others, like your mother, reveled in it."

I started to protest when she took her hand and dragged it through the water, dispelling the image. Another pass showed the little girl was now a woman. I drank in her vision, finding traces of myself in her eyes and her form.

Inari smiled sadly. "You are much like her. Loving and strong, and so stubborn."

"What about my father? Who is he?"

She shook her head, ignoring my question. "I think I slept too long this time. There was a feeling of great sorrow, and she came to me in my dreams, heavy with child. With you."

"What happened to her? Why did she leave me?" I asked, not caring that there was a tremor in my voice.

My grandmother made one final pass with her hand over the water with a laugh. "Look, my child. She never left you. You were her world, and she sacrificed herself to keep you safe."

I was stunned as I watched my dreams appear on the pond's surface. The white fox curled around the red. Protectively, I could tell now. Memories of those dreams washed over me. They always came when I was stressed, and I would wake feeling safe and peaceful.

Tears began to fall from my eyes. "What was she protecting me from?"

"All will soon become clear. But now it is time for you to wake," she said as she lay a gentle kiss on my forehead.

I woke to an untuned motorcycle engine rumbling in my ear. Or, more precisely, Magoo purring as he groomed my hair. Glancing at my watch, I saw I still had time to shower and make the meeting at noon.

I hurried and returned to my room to find another kimono laid out for me—this one in black silk with cranes embroidered in a dark red thread. Thankfully the shoes I found waiting for me were not the traditional geta sandals but a pair of tabi (think mittens for your feet). It was odd to have your big toe separated from the rest, but I soon got used to it.

Thankfully, a traditional belt (or obi) was beside the kimono. So it felt more like a dress and less like a robe. The square sleeves stopped just above my wrists, leaving my hands unencumbered. I twisted and turned to get a better look at it. It felt beautiful, and thankfully my tail had vanished while I slept, so the lines were straight and clean.

Brushing my hair back from my face, I looked closely at my features. Maybe it was wishful thinking, but I could see my mother not only in my eyes but in the line of my jaw and how my hair framed my face. Though my red-and-black locks were nothing like hers in color, I wanted to believe that the texture was the same.

Stepping back, I admired the fit of the kimono. I needed to practice tittering bashfully behind my hand, and I could be a geisha. Laughing at my silliness, I called Magoo to my side and left the room.

Ash waited for me at the bottom of the stairs. His roaming eyes seemed to catalog every inch of me, and I caught my breath when he pulled me into a crushing embrace. Stepping back, he ran his hands up my neck and tangled them into my hair.

"I am so sorry I didn't get there sooner." Regret filled his eyes and his words.

I quirked a smile at him. "I think I held my own."

He drew me into another hug. "You did better than that."

This time, when he stepped back, I could see heat in his eyes that nearly made me melt. His gaze dropped to my mouth, and he began to draw me back in.

"I hope I'm not interrupting anything." We jumped apart at the sound of Melinda Paterson's voice.

Her eyes shot daggers at both of us as she told me the Alpha wanted to see me in his office before the meeting. The tone of her voice was enough to make Magoo and I beat a hasty retreat.

I made my way toward the back of the house, his office next to the exam room. It was decorated as you would expect, with dark paneled walls accented in spots with forest-green wallpaper. A large desk dominated the center of the room, with leather seating. It had not changed in all the years I had known Alpha Benton. The Luna once told me that it was because it was easier to clean fur off leather.

The drapes were drawn over the only window in the room, and it took my eyes a moment to adjust and see that several pack enforcers were standing around a chair that Stefan was bound in. Silver chains wrapped his wrists and ankles while heavier iron ones held him to the chair. What surprised me the most was the ball gag in his mouth. I didn't want to know why they had BDSM paraphernalia around.

"Please have a seat, Tai," the Alpha told me, his Luna standing by his side.

Even though Stefan was trussed up tighter than a Christmas goose, I chose a seat as far from him as far away as possible. As it was, I suddenly understood the term "if looks could kill." His gaze was hot and furious, but he appeared to have recovered from his fall. I refused to look away from him. It was not so much a show of dominance as a refusal to be submissive to his wolf. Magoo helped ease my tension when he cuddled up in my lap.

"Stefan Jorgenson, you are now charged with assault on a person under the protection of this pack. What do you have to say?"

He spat when they removed the ball gag. "That is a lie. This whore tried to seduce me. She told me to meet her at the bluffs."

The Alpha scowled at him. "Watch your language."

His expression softened when he turned to me. "Tai, tell us what happened."

"I had too much on my mind and couldn't sleep. So I walked to the bluffs, where I could sit and think." I paused to sip the water that someone handed me. "I'm not sure how long I sat there before I heard a footstep behind me. The next thing I knew, I was picked up and thrown about ten feet."

Stefan began laughing. "Guess what happened next? This poor pitiful Null you took into your home shifted. She's been lying to you the whole time. She can shift into a fox."

A look of surprise crossed Alpha Benton's face. "Is this true, Tai?"

"It is not," Inari said as she stepped out of a deep shadow in the corner of the room.

The reaction in the room was immediate. Stefan's security began shifting while the Alpha and Luna looked startled. Alpha Benton raised his hand to the enforcers, and they stopped their change mid-shift but maintained their ready stance.

"Are you disputing his claim, Mistress Inari?" the Luna asked.

"Only in so far as his description. Taisetsuna did not turn into a fox. She called her true form to defend herself. She is kitsune." Once again, Inari dressed in a simple kimono. This one was white, with lotus flowers embroidered in pink thread. Her ink-black hair was worn loose and swayed with her movements as she came to stand by my side.

The Alpha began to rise from his chair. "So what this young man is saying is the truth? Tai was never a Null. She only let us believe she was."

Inari shook her head and tsk-tsked at him. "How old was she when she came into your care?"

The Luna was quick to answer. "Maybe eighteen months or younger. She wasn't even speaking well."

"And you think a child that age is capable of the subterfuge you speak about?"

Alpha Benton dropped back into his chair and relaxed. "Of course not. But why were we not able to sense her dual nature? Even after the other children began their changes, she remained defenseless."

"Her abilities were being suppressed. How else would you explain that she had a tail when she first came to you? Did you think it just fell off?"

It was interesting to see the red creep up his cheeks. "The doctors ran tests but could never determine the cause. Once the other children began posing a danger to her, our only thought was to keep her safe."

Settling into the chair next to mine, Inari patted Magoo's head and smiled at him. "And I thank you for that. However, unlike yourself and the other shifters here, kitsune are born and live in their fox forms for the first few years of their lives. But I believe that because Tai's father was not kitsune, this significantly changed her development. One must also take into account the fact that her mother was repressing her abilities."

"How was she able to do that?" Finally, I could ask one of the many questions racing around in my head. We'd get to my sperm donor later.

She took my left hand and turned it over, revealing the scar on my palm. "I believe she used ancient magic to transfer her fox to you as she lay dying. It involves the blood exchange between two people and will cause the one performing the rite to waste away. You would have found little remaining of her."

Releasing my hand, she addressed the rest of the room. "Her fox kept Tai's in a deep sleep. For many years I thought they were both lost to me. I could sense her only after Tai's first awakening ten years ago. I have been watching over her since then. Waiting for the day that she came into her true form."

She rose in a fluid motion and moved to stand before Stefan. "This *sukebe* is the reason for her first and final transformations."

Stefan shrank back as she leaned over him. "I want to both thank you and disembowel you. Time will tell, which I do."

She turned again to the Alpha. "What my granddaughter has told you is the truth. You can ask those that accompanied me and witnessed the whole thing."

"What of the other kitsune? We have thought for many years that they were gone, extinct."

"You are almost correct, Alpha. She is the last kitsune." I saw raw emotion on her face for the first time as her eyes welled with tears.

The Luna cried in pain as if the loss were hers and rushed to embrace Inari. She accepted it gracefully but quickly disengaged herself. "Alpha, did you contact the others as I requested?"

This sudden subject change puzzled me, but the Alpha quickly confirmed he had. He once again turned to address Stefan. "Stefan Jorgenson, I believe the charges brought against you are true and undebatable. Is there anything you would like to say before I pass sentence?"

It was impossible to translate all the vitriol spewing from his mouth, but to sum it up, I was a bitch, the court was a mockery, and the Alpha could perform some physically impossible act on himself.

At a signal from the Alpha, the enforcers fastened the ball gag back into Stefan's mouth and forced him to his feet. "You are hereby outcast from this pack and its territories. You will be put to death if you come within its boundaries at any time. In addition, your wolf will be bound for one year and one day."

While I was happy to know that I'd never have to deal with him again, but I was shocked by the final condition. Binding a shifter's animal was nearly the same as blinding someone. During that time, they would be unable to shift or even commune with their animal side. They would, in effect, be fully human.

Even the gag couldn't muffle his cry of outrage, and I was once again thankful for his restraints. The look on his face as they dragged him from the room promised he would never forget or forgive what was happening here today.

CHAPTER 21

Inari melded back into the shadows and did a vanishing act worthy of Houdini. At the same time, the Luna led me into another room. A large conference table took up most of the area. My stomach grumbled, seeing a large tray of sandwiches occupying a corner table.

"Oh dear, you probably haven't eaten all day," the Luna exclaimed as she fixed a plate for me. Setting it down in front of me, she gestured for me to eat. "Go ahead. Vanessa Rodrik is running late, as usual. So, you have time to put something in your stomach."

She didn't have to tell me twice. I groaned with pleasure as I bit into one that had bologna and potato chips smushed between two pieces of white bread (don't judge).

"See, I remembered this was your favorite." She patted my shoulder. "Now there are other sandwiches on the tray, and I'm going to bring in the coffee. Just take a minute and relax. The day's not over yet."

I stared at the blank face of the 72" flat-screen TV on the opposite wall while nothing more complicated than chewing occupied my mind. I wondered if I was taking a break from reality when I watched a person about the size of a dragonfly flit into the room. They hovered over my nearly empty plate for a moment, trying to reach for one of the chips that had fallen from the sandwich. Nico was right, and I can be a real bitch when I'm hungry, but Magoo was worse, and he refused to concede his right to the scraps that inevitably fell when I ate. So he swatted at the intruder, who tumbled through the air, landing on the carpet. In the blink of an eye, a rather gaunt fellow about my height stood and shook himself. Thick black hair was brushed straight back off his high forehead and his beady black eyes paired with his sharp features made me think of a crow come to life. But his bright Hawaiian shirt and shorts made me think he had just escaped Margaritaville.

"Well, that was uncalled for. I don't eat much in that form, and it's been a long flight," he scolded.

The door the Luna had exited through opened as she wheeled in a large coffee urn. "Puck! Why can't you come through the front door like everyone else?"

He strolled up to the Luna and gave her a big smack on the cheek. "Now where would the fun be in that?"

So this was the mischievous fairy that Shakespeare made famous. I would have to watch my step around him if the stories I'd heard were true. The Luna blushed at his antics and pushed him away. "Would you like some coffee, Tai?"

"Thank you, but you don't have to wait on me. I can get it," I said, jumping to my feet to help while Magoo finished licking the crumbs from my plate.

"Ooh, Tai. What an interesting name. Maybe we could run off together, and you could *tai* me up?" Okay, add *smarmy* to the list of reasons I needed to stay away from him.

Before I could respond, I heard a deep rumbling growl, and a large familiar hand reached around me. Grabbing Puck by the collar of his blindingly bright shirt, Ash picked him up off the ground. But before any harm could befall the miscreant, he shrank back to the small form he'd arrived in and flew to the other side of the table. Regaining his regular size, he brushed at his shirt.

"Really, Avinash, I thought your parents raised you better. This shirt is of the finest silk, spun from the webs of spiders found only in the high Tibetan mountains. It must be washed in the tears of virgins and dried under a full moon."

This statement brought a snort of laughter from me. "And what price did you have to pay to obtain such a treasure?"

"Why, my innocence, of course."

The council members' arrival saved me from any further useless banter. Melinda brought up the rear and shot me a look of loathing. I was making friends left and right today.

The Alpha arrived and immediately claimed the seat at the head of the table. There seemed to be more attendees today than had been present last night. Add to that the council's security detail and Ash looming over me from behind my chair, and the room was starting to feel very confining. Thankfully the Luna opened several of the casement windows directly across from me. The fresh breeze helped ease the claustrophobia that had begun to plague me.

Inari was the last to arrive, and as there were no more seats at the table, she conjured one of her own. Physics tells me that the ornately carved and upholstered throne (yep, a throne) should not have been able to fit into the room. But somehow, she made it happen and settled regally into it. She beckoned, and I thought she was calling me to her side. But it was Magoo who responded, strolling casually across the table and slapping serval participants across the face with both of his tails. I swallowed a laugh when one of the people he targeted was Nico's mother. He jumped into Inari's lap and assumed a relaxed demeanor, though his eyes were ever watchful.

The Alpha looked a bit put out at the theatrics this caused and loudly cleared his throat. "If everyone is ready, let us bring this meeting to order."

Turning to an older woman standing to his right, he asked, "Is he online?"

She gave a sharp nod and tapped on the tablet she held. Instantly, the previously blank screen on the wall lit up, and we connected to the Supe version of Zoom. I was shocked when I realized that the face on the screen was that of the pope himself.

Alpha Benton rose to his feet to address the room. "I thank you all for joining us on such short notice. It has been brought to my attention that we are facing a crisis of epic proportions. What started as a localized outbreak of violence may be linked to the existence of the Life Keys. Mistress Inari, would you like to elaborate?"

She rose from her throne, dislodging Magoo, much to his displeasure. Since walking space was at a premium, she slowly rose and floated gently over the table, landing to the Alpha's left. Turning to the screen, she executed a deep bow and spoke. "As you're all aware, the past months have been a great trial for our human kin. New and exotic diseases are now ravaging their population. Most Supes don't know that these diseases are now beginning to affect our numbers. I believe that the Key of Health is compromised."

I must have had a puzzled look on my face because, well... I had no idea what these keys were.

Puck had selected a seat next to me and leaned in to whisper. "They are talking about the Keys of Life."

On seeing my look of confusion, he continued, "You know how humans always say the key to a good life is to be healthy, wealthy, and wise? Well, those are actual keys."

Before he could explain further, Ash tapped my shoulder to bring my attention back to the room. Looking around, I found every eye on me. The Alpha had a particularly annoyed look on his face. "If we may continue. Inari Okami has assured me that the key entrusted to her is safe. However, Your Holiness, I have asked you here to ensure that the key the Vatican holds is secure. I don't have to explain how catastrophic it would be if all three keys were compromised."

Actually, yes, yes, he did. At least to me. But before I could summon the courage to ask, His Holiness began to speak halting English. "I am afraid that is a matter for the church alone, Alpha Benton. You have yet to explain why you feel the other keys are in danger of being exposed."

Irritation began to bleed into the Alpha's voice. "There have been multiple attacks recently, all aimed at, we believe, obtaining the Key of Wealth. One of our council members has been possessed by what Inari Okami calls an inugami."

The pope frowned at the screen. "I will take all of this under advisement and see to adding additional security to our key. I presume you're doing the same," he commented.

"Of course we are. This council has called in emissaries from other regional governors across the country. We do not intend to let it out of our sight until this matter is resolved."

That would explain the extra people and security in the room. But I had yet to learn why I had to be present. I also wondered how effective the solution was, considering that it included Puck. From what I remember of *A Midsummer Night's Dream*, he was a prankster, not a warrior.

"I must also question what the key, entrusted to our Asian colleagues, is doing in the United States," His Holiness commented.

If I had any questions about how badass my newly found grandmother could be, she wiped them away with her response. Her hair began to whip around her face as if a great wind played with it. The whites of her eyes disappeared into a sea of red, and her mouth opened to show a frightening array of sharp teeth. Her voice echoed and reverberated across the room. "That, sir, is a matter for my kami brethren and me. It is of no concern of yours. I promise you death will visit any who dare threaten it."

Everyone looked startled, and the pope gave a nod of grudging respect. "See that it is so." Then the screen went blank.

Everyone began to talk at once, the sounds rising and falling like the waves on the lake. I tried to make sense of what I was hearing but quickly gave up and sat back. Alpha Benton tried vainly to quiet the voices as the pitch grew higher.

The Luna's growl was the solution to the noise. That and she had partially shifted and now stood nearly seven feet tall. Slamming her hands (paws?) onto the table, she glared around the room. "You will respect my husband and listen to him. Or I'll see each of you out on your asses." Well, that answered the question about how she became the pack Luna. Even the Alpha was a bit cowed by her.

"Thank you, dear. I think I can handle things from here," he soothed her.

Grabbing the coffee cart, she nearly snapped the handle as she pushed it out of the room. I wish I had captured this moment on film as she turned her back to us. She had managed to shred her clothes (a common shifter hazard) except for her apron. So we all watched as one of the scariest wolves walked out sporting a half apron with lace trim.

I raised my hand and waited for the Alpha to notice me. "Sir, may I ask why I'm here? I thought we were here to discuss how to use me to lure the other inugami out and take down their creator."

Inari had resumed her seat and was once again stroking Magoo's back. "There has been a change of plan, granddaughter."

I shook my head. "Okay, so the plan has changed. Then why am I here at all? I know nothing about these life keys or whatever they are."

With a deep sigh, she gently set Magoo on the floor. Folding her hands in her lap, she stared at them and seemed to come to a decision, then raised her head. "While I am proud to see that you are finally coming into your heritage, that brings a certain responsibility. A responsibility that can put your life in danger.

"Many centuries ago, humans began to evolve. In their evolution, their beliefs brought into creation these keys. The first was the Key of Wealth, brought into being by those that had and coveted material possessions. Waves of violence rocked the lands in their search for this key. Disease soon followed, and they became wiser, realizing that the wealth they accumulated without good health meant nothing. These beliefs brought the next two keys into creation—the Key of Health and the Key of Wisdom."

She paused and appeared to gather her thoughts. "Legend says that the person who possessed all the keys would rule the world. Or destroy it. So the keys were dispersed and given to keepers to safeguard them. The kami acquired the Key of Wealth, and I took responsibility for its safety. In my wisdom, I thought it best to break the key apart. I gifted a small part to each of my kitsune, my children, so they might flourish. I foolishly thought this would make finding it more difficult as they scattered across the lands."

A mask of grief settled over her face. "I never took into account their safety, and as I slept, the evil in the world found them. Until only one survived."

Tears glistened in her eyes as she looked at me. "My mother," I whispered.

Straitening her shoulders, she continued, "As each one died, their piece of the key returned to me. I now possess the majority of the key except for one piece. That piece now resides in you, my granddaughter. That is why the inugami have hunted you. They sense the key but don't understand that you do not hold the whole. Only a part."

Of course, Vanessa Rodrick had to question this, as she likes to question everything, primarily where I was concerned.

"So you would have us believe that in all these centuries, no other kitsune produced children? And that Tai is, if you will excuse the pun, the key to all of these problems?" she asked with a smirk on her face.

My grandmother shot Vanessa a look that wiped the vampire's face clean, then began addressing the room again. "My children were very fruitful and multiplied quickly. However, only a zenko or nine-tailed kitsune will breed true. Tai's mother was the only one to obtain that status. The rest died too soon."

The Alpha shot her a sympathetic look. "What happened to the other offspring?"

We all turned as one when the door opened, and Viktor Asmuth walked in. "Yes, Grandmother, why don't you tell the Alpha what became of the rest of your grandchildren."

CHAPTER 22

They stood staring at each other, not blinking. Silenced reigned supreme as we each held our breaths to see who would give in first. Puck did a passable imitation of a cricket until Ash leaned over and flicked the tip of his pointed ear. My eyes were starting to feel dry just watching them.

Inari never blinked but did turn to look at those assembled at the table. "They were not kitsune."

Throwing his arms wide, Viktor was quick to reply. "And only kitsune are worthy of the great Inari Okami's attention."

Leaning on the table, he pointed his finger at her. "Well, let me tell you something, oh great kami. You suck as a grandmother. Tai would have been better off never knowing you. It's your fault the inugami are here, not hers."

The Alpha tried to regain control. "Mr. Asmuth, what brought you here today?"

Viktor turned and made a slight bow to him. "My apologies, Alpha Benton. I wanted to discuss my plan for drawing out the beasts."

The Alpha raised one eyebrow. "You could have called."

The man I now knew was my cousin sort of narrowed his eyes and smiled. "But then I would not have been able to assist Tai. She will need someone to teach her how to use these new abilities she is coming into."

Inari snorted. "And how will you teach her? You are nothing more than the son of a failed alchemist. Your mother always did have dismal taste in men."

He snarled back at her. "More than you, you dried-up old hag. My mother taught me everything she could. But she perished of a broken heart after her husband died, and the only mother she ever knew disowned her."

It was like watching a tennis match. Look at Inari, swivel to look at Viktor and see if he can return her verbal volley, then swivel back again. I needed some popcorn. I must have said that last bit out loud because Puck conjured a whole bowl and pushed the mouthwatering buttered goodness under my nose, but not before grabbing a handful for himself.

"Enough!" Alpha Benton barked. Having regained everyone's attention, he sat back and gestured to Viktor. "What is this brilliant idea?"

Viktor took a deep breath to calm himself while the rest of us (yes, even Inari) waited for him to explain. "I suggest we let Councilman Daecer free."

This statement created a not-so-minor uproar, and this time it was Ash's voice that brought the room to order. Or actually, his roar. I had no idea he could let out such a sound when not in his tiger form. Sexy. But he was still a jerk. "Explain."

"We let Daecer escape and follow him to the others," he pronounced with a shrug.

"What if we lose track of him?" Ash's tone appeared to have a bit of snark when he asked this.

"Then we use Tai to lure them. He is in a heavy trance right now to keep him subdued. It would be easy enough to plant an idea of where they could find her. We keep her under surveillance and grab them when they take the bait."

He walked over to my chair, forcing Ash to move. Much to his displeasure. "In the meantime, I can teach Tai what it is to be kitsune. Perhaps I could help her shift into her fox form."

"But...," I started to protest, but my grandmother held up one hand to silence me.

"Perhaps you are right. Tai may blossom under your tutelage." Her calm gaze was at odds with the verbal assaults we had just witnessed.

I glanced over at Ash, who now stood behind Puck. He looked just as puzzled as I felt. I'd already shifted, and as odd as it sounded, I was confident I could do it again. I just knew it. But glancing around the room, I realized that Ash was the only one present who knew that, besides Inari herself. For some reason, she did not want me to reveal that fact yet.

Viktor bowed his head as though honored by her acquiescence. But not before I saw a flash of satisfaction in his eyes.

The Alpha called a break to the meeting and invited us all to partake of the food set out while he and Viktor met privately to discuss details. I needed to take the opportunity to get Inari to answer some questions. Like why she hid the fact that I had already shifted. But not before Puck pulled me aside.

Puck told me, "Be careful, little girl. There is something about that man that does not sit right with me. I feel as if I have met him before, and though I may play the fool, I have Oberon's ear for a reason."

I surprised even myself when I gave him a quick hug. "Thank you. I appreciate the concern. Now I need to talk with my grandmother."

Turning, I found that she had vanished. Poof. No smoke, no elaborate exit. She and her over-the-top chair (throne) were just gone. Frowning, I looked for Ash and found him standing near the doors as if waiting for me.

"Did you see where my grandmother went?" I asked.

He just shook his head. "No. One minute she was there, and the next, she was gone."

"She's up to something. But what?" I swiveled my head back and forth, looking around, just in case I had missed her.

"I'm not sure. But it is a good idea to keep your shifting to ourselves. It might be to our advantage."

"But what about the others that were at the bluff? Didn't they see my kitsune form?" I worried.

"No. The others were behind us and only saw your cute little tail." He smirked.

I punched him in the shoulder, albeit easier than I would have liked. "Stop it!"

He gave me an innocent look. "Stop what?"

"The flirting. Stop." I felt an overwhelming need to get away before I said something I didn't mean. Or let Ash see the tears that gathered in my eyes. Spinning on my heels, I climbed the stairs to seek sanctuary in my room. But his firm grip on my arm stopped me.

"We need to talk. You and I have a lot to discuss." His face no longer showed humor as he looked at me hard enough to make me squirm.

Alpha Benton calling Ash's name saved me from a conversation I was unsure I wanted to have. Pulling my arm from his grip while he was distracted, I raced up the stairs. Slipping into my room, I closed the door and leaned against it with my eyes closed. That's why I didn't notice Melinda sitting on the bed.

I jumped at the sound of her voice. "I hope you don't think his attention is anything more than a passing fancy."

Squeezing my eyes shut harder did nothing to make her go away. Opening them, I moved farther into the room and found my freshly laundered clothes draped over a chair in the corner. "I have no idea what you're talking about, and if you don't mind, I'd like to get some real clothes on."

She stood and strolled toward the door. "You may have Ash's attention now. Have some fun, but I don't think it will ever go any further. You're just a passing fancy to him. No longer Null, you're finally worth his time."

She opened the door and threw one last salvo at me. "Ash will return to me as soon as he tires of you. He always does when he finishes with his latest toy."

I let myself fall back on the bed as the door slammed. Closing my eyes, I drifted off into a land where nothing had changed. I was still Tai the Null, the paramedic, the introvert with no life. I didn't dream. I was not out long enough to. But I woke to a soft knock on the door.

"Come in," I said around a massive yawn.

Anika peeked her head around the door. "May I come in? I picked up the clothes that you left at the condo."

I waved toward the chair where my other clothes lay. "Just toss them over there."

She did as I asked and then flopped on the bed beside me. "What are you doing?"

"Trying to escape reality."

"How's that working out for you?" she asked.

"Not great." I turned over and looked at her. "When did my life get out of control? All I ever wanted was to escape from all of this drama." Sighing, I flopped onto my back again. "Now I'm the center of it."

Anika pulled a flask out of her pocket and passed it to me. "Try some of this."

Opening the top, I sniffed and smelled notes of ginger and spice. "What is it?"

"It's called a Mumbai Mule."

"Will it help?" I mumbled after taking a large drink from it.

She just shrugged. "It couldn't hurt."

I giggled and passed the flask back to her. "Thanks."

We lay there companionable in silence, passing the flask back and forth. The liquor was strong enough that I could feel my muscles releasing their tension. Then Ash had to go and ruin it.

"Anika, Amma wants you back at the house," he announced, walking into the room. No knock. No "excuse me," just typical Ash arrogance.

As she got up to leave, I grabbed her arm. "Leave the booze."

She tipped the container upside down and shook it. "Sorry, all gone."

"Bummer." I sighed.

I listened as she crossed the room and closed the door gently behind her. I don't know what she thought was going on, but it wouldn't require a closed door.

"We need to talk," Ash said as he sat beside me on the bed.

"Yeah, you said that already. But I don't know what we have to discuss." The alcohol was playing keep-away with my regular filter. "Why don't you run off, find your girlfriend, and talk to her."

"Melinda is not my girlfriend," he shot back.

I propped myself up on my elbows and frowned at him. "Well, you see…right there. That you immediately knew whom I was talking about says that is a lie."

He sighed and ran his hand through his hair. "You're not going to make this easy, are you?"

I had my eyes closed again as I lay back on the bed, and I could feel myself smirk. "Everyone has to have a hobby."

He grabbed me around the waist, picked me up, and set me on his lap. I admit I may have let out a little *peep*, but I kept my cool otherwise. I think.

"I am not going to lie to you. Melinda and I did have a thing, but that is long over," he tried explaining.

I turned to look at him. "Really? Sure didn't look that way the other day at the club."

He had the grace to blush. "Yeah, well. I've been out of sorts since I saw you again. I guess I was trying to get you off my mind."

I raised one brow and snorted. "Pull the other one. It has bells on it."

He sighed and rested his forehead on mine. "Let me tell you a story. A small shifter boy met an adorable toddler just over twenty years ago. One that made his inner tiger purr in contentment. Over the next few years, he couldn't get enough of her. He only ever felt happy in her presence. But then she got hurt by another child, and he had to keep himself from tearing that child apart. Then his parents talked with him and pointed out how fragile that little girl was and how he had to be careful not to make her cry as that other child had." My heart almost broke at such a sad look on his face. "Then they took the little girl to live far away."

"I wasn't that far away," I whispered.

"To a nine-year-old, it might as well have been on the moon." He shifted me in his lap so I could now straddle his legs. "He was so happy when she would come and stay for a day here or there. But he couldn't forget how she had cried when she was hurt. So he tried to stay away. He tried to stay aloof even when she started attending the same school.

"Then came the junior/senior prom, and he had to watch some other boy put his hands on her. That little girl that had grown into a vision wearing a pale yellow dress." I almost fell apart when he put his lips on my neck. "It tore him apart, so much so that he scared the other boy away from her and tried to steal her for himself. They shared a kiss in the back of the gym, and it remained in his mind. But he kept hearing his parents telling him she was so fragile, and he asked his best friend to take her home. Because he wouldn't have been able to control himself if he'd done it."

My face twisted into a sour expression. "And we all know how that turned out."

I shivered as he placed a gentle kiss on my ear. "What you don't know is what Stefan told me when he got back. He said you were so angry that you never wanted to see me again. That you never wanted anything to do with me or the pack again. He said that you wanted me to drop dead."

I pulled away and stared into his eyes. "And you believed him?"

"Why wouldn't I? He was my best friend. It was a long time before I started to see his true colors. But by that time, you had your own life, and I had no place in it."

It seemed like my life was a series of unfinished moments as my door was flung open. Didn't anyone around here know how to knock?

"Mr. Montgomery, the Alpha needs to see you right away," a giant shifter in a Bagha shirt announced.

Ash picked me up and set me on my feet. "Tell him I'll be right down."

Before walking out the door, he placed a quick kiss on top of my head. "This isn't done."

CHAPTER 23

I quickly changed into jeans from the bag Anika had picked up. Hurrying downstairs, I found everybody in an uproar.

I sidled up to Puck and asked. "What is going on?"

My heart immediately clenched at the serious look on his face. "They found O'Sullivan. Or what was left of him."

The Alpha held up his hands, and the room quieted. "I think this news answers our question on the next step. I want to vote to allow Viktor Asmuth to implement his plan and release Daecer in the hope that he will lead us to the person behind this."

The vote, though informal, was unanimous. I could see from the expression on Ash's face that he disagreed with it. But Viktor looked almost smug, and I had to shake off a bad feeling.

Alpha Benton came over to me. "Tai, I'd like you to stay here until we know if this is successful."

I nodded my head in agreement. "Is there anything I can do to help?"

"No. Just stay safe. Your parents volunteered to pick up some of your things at the house since we don't know how long this will take," he replied. "They are going to be releasing Daecer shortly. We will have our best trackers and some of Ash's people on him. Even if this thing does not lead us straight back to its master, we can keep it from killing anyone else."

"So you'll have people following him?" I was curious to know.

He shook his head. "Not in the conventional sense. We'll be using technology this time. Ash's company has a drone they are willing to lend to us. He's going to their headquarters to oversee its deployment. Once it's in the air, we will let the councilman 'escape.'

From there, it is a matter of sending teams out at a safe distance to track him. Once he has led us to his creator, we will send all the teams to eliminate the threat."

Following the Alpha outside, I watched several groups of shifters change into animal forms. Melinda led one group, and the sight of her sleek and muscled cougar made me jealous in a different way. I could finally say I was a Supe, yet I had never felt so useless. They faded silently into the trees as daylight began to fade. Dusk was almost upon us, and I was pulled back into the Alpha's office to watch from a safe distance. It was only a short time when we spied the possessed fae exit from a structure across the way. He slipped through the shadows to a line of four-wheel drive vehicles parked outside. His frustration was palpable as he moved from one to another.

The Alpha laughed and pulled the keys from his pocket. "Those cars are made so they cannot be hot-wired. He'll have to make this journey on foot."

Opening one of his desk drawers, he dropped the keys inside. "Why don't you go upstairs and rest. I know you haven't had much sleep in the last twenty-four hours. I have to coordinate the rest of the teams."

I wanted to protest, but a colossal yawn split my face. Making my way back upstairs, I was struck by how quiet the house quiet had become. There were usually plenty of people, family or pack, coming and going. The silence was a bit unnerving. So I was pleased to find Magoo waiting for me in my room.

"Where did you get off to?"

He didn't reply. He just purred and snuggled into me as I hugged him. Another yawn convinced me to lie down, and I removed my phone and set it on the nightstand. I lay on my back and stared at the ceiling as I ran my hand down Magoo's back. The motion was soothing to me as much as it was to him, and we were both soon asleep.

I don't know how long it was before the ringing of the phone woke me. But it was now fully dark. I grabbed the phone before I was fully awake. "Yeah?"

"Is that any way to answer a phone?" It took me a minute to place the voice.

"Viktor?"

"Yes, dear. It is I. I think you need to come home now," he stated.

"Alpha Benton told me to stay here." My head was still fuzzy, and I was getting confused. "My parents were already there today. Did they forget something?"

"Oh, they're still here. Would you like to talk to your father?" The call was getting creepy, and I shook off the rest of the sleep.

My father came on the line. "You need to come home, dumpling. You need to see this."

Dumpling? My father never called me a dumpling. He hated dumplings. A cold wave washed over me as I remembered that was our family's safe word.

Of course, I had to go and blow it. "Daddy, what's wrong?"

I heard a scuffle before Viktor came back on the line. "Come home, Tai."

"Why? What are you doing there? Are my parents okay?"

"I will explain all once you get here. I'll give you half an hour, and then bad things could start happening." Gone was his happy, smarmy voice. His tone sent shivers down my body.

"But how am I supposed to get there? I've got no car." I hated the whine in my voice.

"Figure it out, or my pets will start on your mother first. Oh, and I hope I don't have to tell you not to call anyone. That could turn out to be very bad for your parents. Buh-bye." He hung up before I could plead anymore.

I had no idea what was going on. But I bet I was going to find out my first impression of Viktor was right. Of course, I had no way of contacting my grandmother. I had a sneaking suspicion I was going to need her.

I turned to shake Magoo out of his sleep but found him watching me intently. His ears were cocked forward, and I had to wonder if he had been able to hear the whole conversation. By the dark look on his ordinarily calm face, yes.

"Magoo, where is Inari?" I asked.

He shook his head. I took that to mean he didn't know, and since he was silent about it, I'd hazard a guess he did not have any way to contact her.

I jumped up and began pacing the room. "Shit. How am I going to get there?"

Magoo stopped his pacing and looked at me. "Office."

It took me a moment. "Of course. The keys to the cars out front. Alpha Benton put them in his desk drawer. Wait, how did you know?"

Magoo just blinked at me.

I grabbed my phone and shoved it into my purse. "Never mind. Let's hope there's no one around to stop us."

Peeking my head out into the hallway, I looked around and listened. The house was silent, and someone had dimmed the lights. We quietly closed the door and made our way soundlessly down the stairs. The first floor was shrouded in shadows, and we took advantage of those as we crept toward the office door. My heart dropped when I tried the door. The knob turned, but the door did not open.

I looked down at Magoo. "I think it's locked."

He surprised me when he backed up and ran at it. Throwing himself at the door, he rammed into it. I hoped he had a hard head. But it seemed to work, and the door popped open. We froze for a moment to make sure no one had heard the noise of cat skull hitting wood.

I didn't dare turn on the lights. The house might be empty, but I knew there would still be patrols around the grounds. Thankfully the moon shed enough light into the room that I could make my way to the desk and only hit my shins once on the furniture. Opening the top drawer, I grabbed the key ring. My breath caught when I pulled it out. I no longer heard the clatter of multiple keys, and I didn't start breathing again until I saw the one lone key remaining on it.

"Let's hope they left one car behind because they didn't need it and not because it's out of service," I whispered like a prayer.

I turned and knelt in front of Magoo. "You need to find Ash, Inari, or someone and let them know what is happening."

He scowled at me. "Come."

"Please, Magoo. I can't run in there without some backup plan."
I decided to play on his vanity. "Please. You're the only one I would
trust to do this." Never mind, he was the only one I had who could
do it.

He deflated a bit. "Careful."

I kissed him on his head. "Yes, I'll be careful."

Getting to my feet, I tried to exude confidence as I walked to
the door. "I just have one quick stop to make."

My errand finished, and I closed the front door to the
Montgomerys' house behind me as gently as possible and took stock
of my surroundings. The good news was there was one car remaining
out front. The bad news was it was a red Porsche 911 Carrera. Not
precisely a stealthy ride. I had hoped for some a little less conspicu-
ous. My indecision nearly did me in when I saw two shifters coming
toward me. With confidence I didn't feel, I made my way toward to
sports car as if it belonged to me.

"Ms. Jotun! Where are you going?" the taller of the two called
out.

I turned around and gave them the best puppy-dog eyes I could.
"I need to go help my parents. Their car broke down."

The other shifter looked skeptical. "The Alpha gave you permission to drive his car?"

Thinking fast, I held up the keys I had "borrowed." "I have the
keys. See?" Not a lie. I didn't elaborate on how I got them.

They looked at each other and seemed to come to a decision.
"Be careful. If anything happens, we never saw you."

The smile that lit my face was genuine. "Oh, I'll drive like my
grandmother was in the car with me." They didn't need to know who
my grandmother was.

I waited until they had rounded the building before opening
the car door. The rich smell of the leather interior threatened to make
me swoon, and I relished the feel of the seat as I slid into it. However,
the multitude of gauges and buttons nearly gave me a fit. I missed
my car. It was as essential as could be. Start the car and go; stop the

car and get out. Avoid potholes unless you want to bounce up and hit the headliner.

I silently prayed to whatever gods were listening and turned the key. If the dashboard had not lit up, I wouldn't have even known the car was running; it was that smooth. Putting it into gear (did I forget to mention it was a manual transmission), I eased out of the parking spot and tried not to grind the gears as I headed out of the pack compound. Thankfully, we were close to the interstate, and I was racing toward home within minutes.

I didn't even pretend to try and follow any of the rules of the road; all I cared about was making it home in the allotted time. Speed limits were not even a suggestion to me in this car. Thankfully, traffic was relatively light as I headed south toward the city. I wove in and out, the other vehicles barely a blur. I swung onto the feeder ramps at dizzying speed and through the curves as if glued to the road. I wouldn't have even attempted them in my car for fear of tipping over.

Within two blocks of my destination, the streets became strangely quiet, and there seemed to be a darkness that settled over everything. Just as it had the night, we fought the beasts. I blame that on the few little mishaps I had with the car. It should be okay if the shrubs I ran over didn't leave debris in the undercarriage. Or it would have if I hadn't cut a corner too sharp and driven through a row of trash cans left out for tomorrow's pickup.

I may have jumped the curb when I reached the house. Killing the engine, I sat and stared at my home. Whether from the unnatural gloom or something else, it looked deserted. Maybe they were all sitting in the dark, waiting. With a few minutes to spare, I quickly got out of the car and headed toward the backyard.

Creeping around the perimeter, I noticed all the plants that Uka had sown were dead. A dim light showed out of the kitchen window, but the drapes were drawn, and I couldn't see anything when I pulled myself up to the windows. Backing away, I braced myself to open the back door. But before I could do it, a hand grasped my arm. Spinning, I found the bartender from the night of the party standing too close for comfort.

A sneer crossed his face. "The boss wants to see you."

CHAPTER 24

Wrenching my arm from his grasp, I made my way through the back door. My breath caught when I saw Dunker and Sunreaver holding guns on my parents, who were tied to the kitchen stools.

I ran over and gave Sunreaver a solid kick in his leg. "What the hell are you doing? Put that thing down before I tell your mother about you!"

All I got for my efforts was a sneer and a laugh from both of them. The smell of wet dogs and decay washed over me, and I found the only thing scarier than a mountain troll was one that an inugami possessed.

I backed away and ran to my parents. "Are you okay?"

My mother gave me her bravest smile. "I'm fine. But they roughed up your dad a bit."

Looking at him, I could see his eyes swollen shut, and his jaw was at an odd angle. "Daddy!"

"Such touching concern. But so misplaced." Viktor's voice had me spinning around, fox fire in hand.

Instinct took over, and I threw the fireball straight at his chest. But he reached out and caught it. He then played with it, tossing it from one hand to another. "Your loyalty is misplaced. Really, who are these people to you?"

"They are my parents!" I hissed as I advanced on him.

I ducked when he threw the fox fire back at me and listened as it hit one of my cousins. Sunreaver, I thought, as he cursed a blue streak.

"You mean your adoptive parents, don't you?" He laughed.

I narrowed my eyes at him. "They are my parents. Those people who participated in my creation were nothing more than sperm donor and incubator. Hank and Rachel Jotun are my parents."

All signs of amusement fell from his face. "Yet they contributed nothing to your inherent abilities or DNA. Only your true parents did that."

Shaking my head, I moved to get a clearer view of Viktor Asmuth. "You already know who my mother was. What is it to you who the man was who supplied the sperm?"

In a fit of what I saw as utter madness, he let out a high-pitched giggle and slapped his leg. "Oh my goodness. This is going to be even better than I dreamed." Pulling himself to his full height, he affected a stern expression, affecting a deep, resonant voice; he held one hand out to me. "Tai, I am your father."

"No, you're not," I protested vigorously. "Inari would have told me."

He came over and stood mere inches away from me. Grasping my jaw in his hand, he forced me to look into his eyes. "Grandmother never has been one to lay all her cards out on the table."

I tried pulling away, but his grip was too firm. "So my grandfather was a failed alchemist, and his son, half kitsune?"

He pushed me away roughly. "My father was strigoi. He wasted his life pursuing alchemy to overcome his heritage. He was a fool."

"What is a strigoi?" This is what I get for sleeping through my Myths, Legends, and Supernaturals class.

"Why, my dear, strigoi are vampires. Information you really should learn. Now that you know you are a quarter vampire."

I shuddered. "No. Not possible. The smell of blood makes me nauseated. It is the one thing I have problems with at work."

Viktor shook his head. "There is so much I must teach you. Strigoi don't feed on blood. That is so déclassé. No, strigoi are what some people refer to as psychic vampires. We feed on others' life force or energy."

He chuckled at my blank expression. "Do you like to go out to clubs and dance?"

"Sometimes," I replied cautiously.

"How many times have you come home feeling more energized than when you left? Do your friends seem to tire more quickly than you? At work, are you more focused, while others seem disoriented." He watched me closely while asking these questions.

I cast my mind back, remembering those times I had kept partying long after my friends had left. Or the time our unit assisted the fire department when a large apartment building caught fire. I felt energized as we evaluated each casualty. On the other hand, my partner immediately fell asleep once we returned to our quarters. But I spent the rest of the night playing video games.

I refused to acknowledge his point. "Maybe a little."

He laughed straight in my face. "Oh, Tai, don't ever play poker. You don't have the face for it. But I can teach you how to mask that better."

He clapped his hands and rubbed them together while a manic gleam lit his eyes. "I have so much to teach you. Once you gain your kitsune form, the world will be ours."

I decided to play along and hope that Magoo had been able to get a message to Ash or anyone. "Why is that?"

He grasped my face again between his hands. "Because once you have the Key of Wealth, we will live a life of luxury."

This time, I was able to pull away from him. "How do you expect us to do that?"

"Why, through Verge, of course. Once you have the Wealth Key in your possession and join me, I will be successful beyond my dreams. I mean, our dreams. Not only will we be able to live the high life, but all the energy that the customers produce will keep us young forever."

Despite the insanity I saw in his eyes, I had to ask, "How did you create the inugami? Vampires don't wield magic."

"Do not underestimate me, daughter," Viktor snapped. "I have learned much over the years, and you will do well to remember that."

He bestowed a look of pride on Dunker and Sunreaver. "If you will forgive my saying, they are my greatest creation. They have helped me infiltrate places I would not have been able to. I learned valuable information through them, which is the best currency." His gaze was appraising. "Perhaps one day, you will take their place. You have the potential to be even more valuable."

Stalling him, I asked, "Why did you send them after me?"

"That was pure dumb luck, my dear. I knew who you were the minute I saw you. You have your mother's mannerisms, and I recognized the charm on your wrist. It was the same one she always wore.

"You almost caught me when you outed Daecer. I actually knew Shakespeare. But I spent many years perfecting this persona and honing my acting abilities. Puck nearly gave the game away. I was sure he had recognized me from when I traveled with the bard."

I could tell he was getting annoyed, which was both good and bad. Angry people make mistakes. But they are also unpredictable.

He changed subjects so quickly my head spun. "You know, Grandmother lied to you. The keys did not return to her when the other kitsune died. As each key lost its host, it was broken into equal pieces and dispersed to the surviving kitsune. Until your mother was the last one, she possessed the whole key." I could see his facade begin to crack.

His crazed eyes bore into mine. "I would have given Nasuki the world if she had just used the key. But she was too loyal to Inari and felt that keeping the key safe was the noble thing to do. Stupid girl." Turning, he punched a hole into the wall.

Extracting his hand, he shook it, sending blood and pieces of drywall flying. "Nasuki was of no use to me without the key. But I was truly fond of her, so I sealed her into a room when she found out she was pregnant. I kept her fed and healthy, draining just enough energy so it was difficult to rebel against the confinement. I planned to take you once you were weaned and leave her there. I could not bring myself to kill her like I had the others."

"You see how merciful I was, and what did I have to show for it?" he pleaded with me. But I backed up until I hit a solid wall of troll muscle. "She ran at the first opportunity, taking you with her."

Father or not, the man was batshit crazy. I'm unsure what my response would have been had I not heard a noise from outside, and he must have seen it in my face. I guess he was right; I should never play poker.

Several things seemed to happen at once. Viktor looked all at once sad and resigned. "I can see now that you are your mother's daughter too much. I'm sorry, my dear. If you're not with me, you are against me." From there, everything appeared to slow down. He thrust his left hand forward, and I could sense the magic gathering in the air. A spot of light grew from his palm, and I watched as it gathered strength and began to shoot toward me. I'm not ashamed to say I froze in fear.

Bands of iron wrapped around my shoulders, and I was sure I was about to light up like Fourth of July fireworks. But at the last second, I was spun around. I saw Sunreaver looking back at me, shielding me from the lightning. The shock of the fox fire that hit him before must have allowed him to regain some control, and in a final act of sacrifice, he saved me from being killed. I knew the moment it hit his back. His eyes widened and then rolled back into his head. He took me down with him as he fell. But the descent was slow enough to let me grab the .380 Ruger from my waistband. Rolling away to keep from being pinned under him, I raised the gun I had snuck out of my parents' room earlier and aimed.

My father once told me a person that carries a large gun is overcompensating. The most important thing was to be comfortable with your firearm and know how to shoot it. He ensured I knew how, and the Ruger was small and light enough to hide when concealed in my waistband. You can say one thing about using human technology: few Supes can survive a shot to the head. Thankfully Viktor was not one of them. A well-placed shot between the eyes ended the life of my birth father. I'm sure a trained psychiatrist would have a field day with me, as I felt no emotion when I watched him fall.

As soon as I knew he wasn't getting up again, I dropped to my knees to assess Sunreaver's condition. It wasn't good. I locked away my emotions and put on my professional persona. Grabbing a towel draped on the sink, I tried staunching the flow of blood that was beginning to cover my floor. Dunker had dropped like a rock when I shot Viktor, as the inugami possessing him was set free, but he rallied quickly. Sensing my intentions, he ripped off his shirt and handed it to me to add to the towel. It still wasn't enough. I directed him to my bathroom to get more towels as Sunreaver opened his eyes.

"I done good tonight. Right, Cousin Tai?" he whispered.

"You did great. You're my hero. Just stay still and let me take care of you. Everything is going to be okay." I choked up as I reassured him.

I heard steps pounding up the stairs from the back door. In moments I was forced away from Sunreaver as more qualified people began to work over him. I may be a great paramedic in the human world, but I knew little about Supe physiology. I hovered over the witches I knew were from Bagha by their shirts. Warm light warred with the gaping wound, trying to force it closed. But it was too little, too late, and I watched my cousin die on the kitchen floor.

I would have dropped to my knees if Ash had not been there to catch me. Burying my face in his shirt, I gave in to the stress of the night and soaked it with my tears. Once spent, I turned my head and observed as Dunker mourned over the body of his lost brother. The witches had moved on to my father, and the swelling in his face went down as I watched. My mother had been freed from her restraints and hovered around him.

Soft fur tickled my ankles as Magoo materialized and wound around them. His purring volume ramped up until that was the only sound I heard. It worked as a tonic until I finally pulled away from Ash and regained my composure.

I refused to look at the body that used to be Sunreaver. I walked around him and went to Dunker, hugging him as hard as possible. I'm not sure he even felt it, but he absently patted me on the back.

"Mama will be so proud. Sunreaver died a hero," he rumbled.

He deserved a little dignity in his death, so I went to the linen closet and got a sheet to cover his body. Putting my arm around Dunker's waist again, we stood there looking at the draped form. I nearly wet myself when I saw a ball of pure white light lift from Sunreaver's chest area and float through the ceiling.

Ash had come up beside me, and I asked him, "Did you see that?"

"See what?" The look on his face was enough to tell me he hadn't.

"I think I just watched his soul ascend to heaven." Wonder filled me at the thought.

He gently ran his hand over my hair. "Do trolls have a heaven?"

I gave him a shaky smile. "I'm not sure. But wherever good trolls go when they die, I know that is where he has gone."

I leaned into him and let myself gain strength from his presence while we pondered that age-old question. "Let's go into the living room and get out of everyone's way." He went from stroking my hair to rubbing my back.

It took me a moment to realize even more people had filled my tiny kitchen. Besides Ash and his Bagha crew, I saw Nico trying to make his way to me. Several hulking shifters stood guard by the back door and nearly tossed him out. The rest of the Montgomerys trailed in after him and immediately went to help the witches working on my parents. Magoo took it seriously when I asked him to call in the cavalry.

Ash led me to the other room and settled me on the sofa. A large cup of hot tea materialized in my hand. Taking a sip, I nearly gagged on all the sugar they had put in it. It felt like my teeth started to rot.

Sitting next to me, Ash kept touching me as if to reassure himself I was okay. Letting his nearness and the hot tea settle me, I sat back and closed my eyes. They popped open again when I heard the front door crash open as Alpha Benton entered the room. Things were about to get awkward.

"Why is my Porsche parked in the front yard?" he bellowed.

EPILOGUE

Six weeks later

I leaned against the airplane window as it taxied to the gate. I was arriving home with some trepidation. The meaning of home would change as I had no intention of ever setting foot into my little bungalow again. That part of my life was over. I had come to terms with that during the six weeks I had spent with my parents in Florida. I had yet to come to terms with my parents' insistence on moving back to Milwaukee. We had agreed to sell the house, and my parents happily accepted an offer from Alpha Benton to live on the pack grounds. They would be following me back in the next couple of weeks. I had also received one to stay there until I found a new place to call home.

We had left for Florida right after Sunreaver's funeral. The Alpha had provided a place for his cairn in honor of his bravery and sacrifice. We had all helped build it, piling rock after rock on top, then participated in a proper trollish farewell. It reminded me of a Maori Haka, with lots of chest slapping and chanting. It was both fierce and touching. Dunker was correct; his mother and the rest of the clan were proud that his brother had died a hero.

Inari had been suspiciously quiet. The only contact I'd had with her had been in one of my dreams. So many questions were left unanswered, the primary of which was that Viktor was my father. Did she know? Was my mother his captive or his consort? Had he been responsible for other kitsune deaths? I truly wanted to know these things, but she refused to answer. The only words she spoke were, "You are ready," and then she kissed me on the mouth. That was strange enough, but worse was the pain that woke me. Rushing to the bathroom, I looked in the mirror and stuck out my tongue. To my horror, I now sported a piercing. But instead of a gold ball, a gold key adorned it. It took me most of six weeks to learn to talk without lisping, and the stupid thing kept clicking when it hit the back of my teeth.

Alpha Benton was providing a pack member, a genuine fox shifter, to help me become comfortable with my new form. The council decided it would be best to keep my true nature a secret for now. At least until the Key of Health could be tracked down and hopefully retrieved. For now, the story would be that I was a fox shifter.

There was one good thing that came out of all this. Being an old villainous douchebag was quite profitable for Viktor. The council had voted that his estate would go to me as his daughter. Further testing had shown that I did possess strigoi blood, but that is another tale. It cemented his claim that I was his daughter, and to the victor go the spoils, so they say. That meant I was now the proud owner of a Supernatural nightclub and heiress to more money than I could have ever hope to make in ten of my lifetimes.

I had taken Nico on as a partner in the club, as I had no desire to run it. He was over the moon since Peter hadn't taken their breakup well and fired him on the spot. Now he was planning many events, most of which surrounded him. But he was happy, the club was doing well, and I never had to step foot in it again if I didn't want to.

I even repaired all the "minor" scratches on the Alpha's Porsche. He graciously accepted my apologies and admitted he might have done the same thing in my place.

As for Ash, the butterflies in my stomach felt like they were doing the rumba. He had offered to pick me up once my plane landed. We talked almost every night during my absence. But there was a part of me that just couldn't let go of the hurt he had caused. And I did blame him for the past ten years. Stefan may have instigated the problems, but Ash should have known me better and reached out. You might argue that I should have known better than to believe Stefan. But Ash's actions that night so long ago overrode any past we'd had.

I stalled as long as I could before finally grabbing my carry-on from the overhead storage and following my fellow sardines out of the can they called a plane. Making my way to the luggage claim area, I kept my eyes open for Ash. It wasn't until I had grabbed my bag and pushed my way out of the sea of humans that I caught sight of him.

He wore a black collared Bagha shirt molded to his chest and arms. Paired with form-fitting dark blue jeans and cowboy boots, it took all my strength not to drool, especially with the way his eyes seem to drink me in. I stood as still as a gazelle in a predator's gaze while he strolled up to me.

Stopping within inches of me, he stared hungrily at me. "Hi."

"Hi," I whispered, leaning into him.

He met me halfway and laid a gentle kiss on my lips. But I was hungry for more, and it soon became a contest as to whom could suck the other one's soul out of their body first.

Reluctantly coming up for air, he grabbed my bag with one hand and my arm with his other. Guiding me through the multitude of people, he led me out to the pickup area.

"They let you park here?" I asked, knowing how strident the airport authority was about unoccupied vehicles.

He gave me a smug little smile. "Not quite."

I looked around but didn't see any cars that appeared to be waiting for us. Ash motioned for me to look toward the airport entrance. My jaw hit the ground when I saw a speck of purple making its way through the traffic toward us.

"Is that..." It was hard to get the words out of my mouth.

A huge smile split his face. "Is that what?" He still loved teasing me.

Refusing to take my eyes off the car as it got closer, I grabbed his hand. "My car. My purple baby. But how?"

"How, indeed?"

He rocked back as I threw myself into his arms. "I may have pulled a few strings and had some body work done on it."

Covering his face in kisses, I nearly swooned when my restored Suzuki pulled up to the curb. It was followed closely by a black sedan. A short but well-muscled shifter jumped out of the X90 and tossed the keys to Ash. He then turned and presented them to me. "I did make one modification to it."

I barely heard him as I ran my hands over the car. Not only had the roof been fixed, but it looked like every ding and spot of rust was gone. "What was that?"

He chuckled. "I had a roll bar put in."

The End

ABOUT THE AUTHOR

With a lifelong interest in comparative religions, folklore, and mythology, the author now lives in Milwaukee with her musician husband. Their household includes two dogs, two cats, and way more drums than any one person needs.

Milton Keynes UK
Ingram Content Group UK Ltd.
UKHW010624041223
433752UK00001B/221